Perdita

and the Christmas People

Peter Hunt

Perdita
and the
Christmas People

or

What Happened at Tolpuddle

SE

Peter Hunt's **Perdita** series, first published by Shakspeare Editorial,
UK, 2021

Novel three ~ *Perdita and the Christmas People, or What Happened at Tolpuddle*
ISBNs   pbk 978-1-8383041-7-1
                ebk 978-1-8383041-8-8

Design and typesetting www.ShakspeareEditorial.org

Contents

24 DECEMBER, CHRISTMAS EVE

25 DECEMBER, CHRISTMAS DAY

26 DECEMBER, BOXING DAY

27 DECEMBER

28 DECEMBER

29 DECEMBER

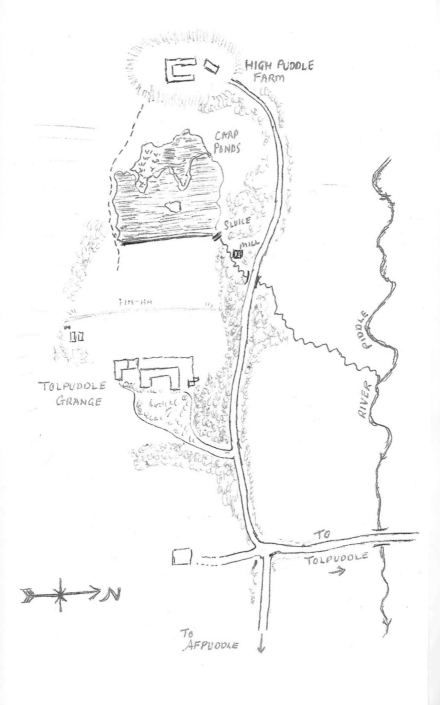

HIGH PUDDLE FARM

CARP PONDS

SLUICE

MILL

HA-HA

TOLPUDDLE GRANGE

TO TOLPUDDLE

TO AFPUDDLE

RIVER PIDDLE

N

A Note on Places

Tolpuddle is a real place in the real world, and a nice place it is too, and everything in this book about the Tolpuddle Martyrs is true. But the Tolpuddle in this book is really only a place of the imagination, and Tolpuddle Grange, with its carp ponds and woods and dam and attics and cellars, is a place of the imagination as well. It is not to be confused with the real and wonderful old houses nearby – Tolpuddle Manor, down by the church, or Southover House, across the water meadows, or the much haunted Athelhampton House, just up the river. It may possibly owe more to Southover House than the others, because of a happy holiday spent there, and we would like to thank its owners for unwittingly letting us borrow the spirit of the place, if not its actual stones and trees (and telephone).

A Note on People

A lot of authors begin their books by saying that this is only fiction, and that nobody in it is real, in case anyone gets upset. In this case, I can only repeat the words of the great detective writer, Margery Allingham: '*Every character in this book is a careful portrait of a living person, each one of whom has expressed himself or herself delighted not only with the accuracy but with the charity of the delineation. Any resemblance to any unconsulted person is therefore accidental.*'

21 DECEMBER

Prelude

In Which There are Bits of Books

Perdita sat in front of her biggest bookshelf and counted in her head the number of books that began with the people in them going on holiday.

Daddy would come down to breakfast and say something like, 'Mummy and I have to go away on an expedition to Inner Mongolia, so we can't go on our usual holiday to Little Shrimpton. I hope you don't mind staying with your Uncle Sholto and your five cousins at his nearly ruined old castle.' Or they would be in the back of the car as Daddy (always Daddy) drove over a hill, and there would be the wide sandy beach (always empty) and the big house where they were staying for their holidays, with their seven cousins. Or they would be arriving by train at a country station where their friends (three of them) would be waiting with a pigeon to tell their other friends (three more) that they would be arriving at their camping place very soon.

Whichever it was there would soon be lots of cousins or friends running around in the book, and sometimes there were so many that she had to stop reading and write down who they were so she wouldn't forget. Daddy said he had the same trouble with Russian novels (although Perdita knew that this was not exactly true because she had looked into Daddy's Russian novels and had decided that the problem was that the names were *very* long.) That was one thing about the books about holidays: the people in them generally had very short names, that were easy to remember, and it was also easy to remember what each one was like. There was always a very Strong and Noble boy, who was the leader, and another big boy who wasn't very bright and might also be a bully; there was smaller boy (usually with glasses) who was very clever, and there was a *smaller* boy who was always eating chocolate and falling off things or into things. Then there was always a very adventurous girl who was as good as a boy at climbing and sailing, and there was another girl who looked after everybody and did the cooking; and a smaller girl who was very dreamy; and the smallest girl who was always eating chocolate and falling off things or into things.

Perdita thought that none of her cousins were like any of those, but equally, she wouldn't like to have to write a book with them in it, and to explain to other people who they all were.

Usually at Christmas they went to see one of the Aunts (she had three) and some of her cousins (she had five altogether if you counted the babies), or one or two of the Aunts came to them for Christmas Day or Boxing Day, or they went to Granny and Grandprof's house. But this year they were all going to the same place – a huge country house – a Grange, no less – that Granny and Grandprof had taken for the week over Christmas – and this had led to a lot of research.

Daddy had been looking up legends and folk tales about Dorset, because that's where the Grange was, and he wanted to be able to sit in front of one of the blazing log fires – proper log fires, Perdita thought, always blazed – and tell them to Perdita and Sebastian and Dulcie and the cousins. Mummy had only wondered aloud whether telling ghostly stories about strange happenings in big old creepy houses was a good idea when you were actually sleeping in a big old creepy house.

Sebastian had been looking at maps – Grandprof had lent him a handful – to see if there was a river at Tolpuddle (where the Grange was), or a railway, or ancient earthworks and old airfields, or even a beach, because Dorset was beside the sea. There was a river, but there wasn't a railway, but there were plenty of earthworks and large areas marked with flat red arrows on the map where you couldn't go at certain times without being shot at by the Army, who used those bits of land to practice shooting at things. And there was a beach, if you didn't mind driving to it.

But Perdita had been reading about Granges and big old mansion houses, and she knew a lot about *them*. So while Mummy had been in conference with Granny and Aunty Cass on the phone about food, and had been sorting out cold weather clothing and wet weather clothing and negotiating how many bags they were allowed to take with them, Perdita had been checking her library.

Today was the 21st December, which, Sebastian had told her, was usually the Winter Solstice and the shortest day of the year, except that this year it was the day *before* the shortest day, because sometimes it worked out that way. Tomorrow they were going to finish loading the car and drive to Tolpuddle, which sounded exciting, but there was one serious drawback. Travelling on the shortest day of the year meant that when their dancing friends, Tim and Dan and Emma and Dancing Perdita, would be meeting on the Tump outside their house, and having dances and a bonfire for the Solstice, and a headless horse was supposed to come galloping out of the nether world, she, Perdita, would probably be sitting in a traffic jam somewhere, and *not* dancing or watching headless horses. Daddy had said that he could guarantee that there wouldn't be any traffic jams, but that Tolpuddle sounded like just the place for a headless horse. And so everybody had decided that they could dance on the Tump any day, and that a house with ten bedrooms and a playroom, and a library, and attics, and a games room in the cellar and tennis courts and carp ponds, whatever they were, was something that you simply had to go and play in, whether it was the shortest day or not.

And so Perdita was sitting on the floor of her bedroom at home in front of her biggest bookcase, with several books open around her. She had already unpacked her clothes from her suitcase and repacked them in her backpack, because she had worked on that you could get more books in the suitcase. Mummy had said, in her way of saying things that she knew were not actually worth saying, that Tolpuddle Grange did actually have a library all of its own, so there might be books in it, but Perdita suspected that it might not be a library with the Right Books in it, and so she was taking an emergency supply.

She'd seen a picture of Tolpuddle Grange which seemed, like the name, to be promising. But she couldn't decide whether the place was going to be bright and cheerful, as when Little Lord Fauntleroy arrived at Dorincourt Castle, and it whether it was going to be three miles from the gate to the house.

The carriage rolled on and on between the great, beautiful trees which grew on each side of the avenue and stretched their broad, swaying branches in an arch across it. Cedric had never seen such trees,— they were so grand and stately, and their branches grew so low down on their huge trunks. He did not then know that Dorincourt Castle was one of the most beautiful in all England; that its park was one of the broadest and finest, and its trees and avenue almost without rivals. But he did know that it was all very beautiful. He liked the big, broad-branched trees, with the late afternoon sunlight striking golden lances through them. He liked the perfect stillness which rested on everything. He felt a great, strange pleasure in the beauty of which he caught glimpses under and between the sweeping boughs—the great, beautiful spaces of the park, with still other trees standing sometimes stately and alone, and sometimes in groups. Now and then they passed places where tall ferns grew in masses, and again and again the ground was azure with the bluebells swaying in the soft breeze. Several times he started up with a laugh of delight as a rabbit leapt up from under the greenery and scudded away with a twinkle of short white tail behind it. Once a covey of partridges rose with a sudden whir and flew away, and then he shouted and clapped his hands.

And of course there would be lots of jolly servants lined up to meet them.

Or maybe it would be dark and frightening as when poor Mary Lennox arrived at Misselthwaite Manor after a long long train journey through the night.

On and on they drove through the darkness, and though the rain stopped, the wind rushed by and whistled and made strange sounds.

The road went up and down, and several times the carriage passed over a little bridge beneath which water rushed very fast with a great deal of noise. Mary felt as if the drive would never come to an end and that the wide, bleak moor was a wide expanse of black ocean through which she was passing on a strip of dry land.

'I don't like it,' she said to herself. 'I don't like it,' and she pinched her thin lips more tightly together.

The horses were climbing up a hilly piece of road when she first caught sight of a light. Mrs Medlock saw it as soon as she did and drew a long sigh of relief.

'Eh, I am glad to see that bit o' light twinkling,' she exclaimed. 'It's the light in the lodge window. We shall get a good cup of tea after a bit, at all events.'

It was 'after a bit,' as she said, for when the carriage passed through the park gates there was still two miles of avenue to drive through and the trees (which nearly met overhead) made it seem as if they were driving through a long dark vault.

They drove out of the vault into a clear space and stopped before an immensely long but low-built house which seemed to ramble round a stone court. At first Mary thought that there were no lights at all in the windows, but as she got out of the carriage she saw that one room in a corner upstairs showed a dull glow.

The entrance door was a huge one made of massive, curiously shaped panels of oak studded with big iron nails and bound with great iron bars. It opened into an enormous hall, which was so dimly lighted that the faces in the portraits on the walls and the figures in the suits of armour made Mary feel that she did not want to look at them. As she stood on the stone floor she looked a very small, odd little black figure, and she felt as small and lost and odd as she looked.

Or they might get there in the dark, and the house would be locked, and there would be nothing to eat.

The man who drove tem from the station unlocked the door and went in and set his lantern on the table.

'Got e'er a candle?' said he.

'I don't know where anything is.' Mother spoke rather less cheerfully than usual.

He struck a match. There was a candle on the table, and he lighted it. By its thin little glimmer the children saw a large bare kitchen with a stone floor. There were no curtains, no hearth rug. The kitchen table from home stood in the middle of the room. The chairs were in one corner, and the pots, pans, brooms, and crockery in another. There was no fire, and the black grate showed cold, dead ashes.

As the cart man turned to go out after he had brought in the boxes, there was a rustling, scampering sound that seemed to come from inside the walls of the house.

'Oh, what's that?' cried the girls.

'It's only the rats,' said the cart man. And he went away and shut the door, and the sudden draught of it blew out the candle.

'Oh, dear,' said Phyllis, 'I wish we hadn't come!' and she knocked a chair over.

'ONLY the rats!' said Peter, in the dark.

And when they got everything organised, and they went off to their bedrooms, there might be strange noises in the night, and a mad woman in the attic.

I started wide awake on hearing a vague murmur, peculiar and lugubrious, which sounded, I thought, just above me. I wished I had kept my candle burning: the night was drearily dark; my spirits were depressed. I rose and sat up in bed, listening. The sound was hushed.

I tried again to sleep; but my heart beat anxiously: my inward tranquillity was broken. The clock, far down in the hall, struck two. Just then it seemed my chamber-door was touched; as if fingers had swept the panels in groping a way along the dark gallery outside. I said, 'Who is there?' Nothing answered. I was chilled with fear.

All at once I remembered that it might be Pilot the house dog who, when the kitchen door chanced to be left open, not unfrequently found his way up to the threshold of Mr. Rochester's chamber: I had seen him lying there myself in the mornings. The idea calmed me somewhat: I lay down. Silence composes the nerves; and as an unbroken hush now reigned again through the whole house, I began to feel the return of slumber. But it was not fated that I should sleep that night. A dream had scarcely approached my ear, when it fled affrighted, scared by a marrow-freezing incident enough.

This was a demoniac laugh—low, suppressed, and deep—uttered, as it seemed, at the very keyhole of my chamber door. The head of my bed was near the door, and I thought at first the goblin-laugher stood at my bedside—or rather, crouched by my pillow: but I rose, looked round, and could see nothing; while, as I still gazed, the unnatural sound was reiterated: and I knew it came from behind the panels. My first impulse was to rise and fasten the bolt; my next, again to cry out, 'Who is there?'

Something gurgled and moaned. Ere long, steps retreated up the gallery towards the third-storey staircase: a door had lately been made to shut in that staircase; I heard it open and close, and all was still.

Perdita looked up at her bedroom window. Outside, it was already dark. All December and cold and clouds blowing. Perhaps at Tolpuddle there would be forbidden rooms, and the wind blowing from the moors.

But as she was listening to the wind she began to listen to something else. She did not know what it was, because at first she could scarcely distinguish it from the wind itself. It was a curious sound—it seemed almost as if a child were crying somewhere. Sometimes the wind sounded rather like a child crying, but presently Mistress Mary felt quite sure this sound was inside the house, not outside it. It was far away, but it was inside. She turned round and looked at Martha.

'Do you hear anyone crying?' she said.

Martha suddenly looked confused.

'No,' she answered. 'It's th' wind. Sometimes it sounds like as if someone was lost on th' moor an' wailin'. It's got all sorts o' sounds.'

'But listen,' said Mary. 'It's in the house—down one of those long corridors.'

And at that very moment a door must have been opened somewhere downstairs; for a great rushing draft blew along the passage and the door of the room they sat in was blown open with a crash, and as they both jumped to their feet the light was blown out and the crying sound was swept down the far corridor so that it was to be heard more plainly than ever.

So, Perdita thought, you never knew. There might be pictures on the wall, and the happy voices of children who used to live there. And they might appear to you and you wouldn't know if they were dreams or not. And all that was to say nothing of the secret panel in the library, and the secret passage in the cellar.

She picked up a green-covered book, and opened it at the title page. There was a quotation, and she read it, whispering: '"Dark by teatime and sleeping indoors. Nothing ever happens in the winter holidays."'

She closed the book, put it carefully into her suitcase, and, feeling very cheerful, went downstairs to tea.

22 DECEMBER

Chapter 1

In Which Perdita finds a Pond and Dulcie finds a Ha-Ha

'Are we nearly there?' Dulcie said.

'Another three hours,' Daddy said.

Mummy looked in the driving mirror in time to catch the look on Dulcie's face.

'Daddy's just joking,' she said. 'Two more minutes.'

She turned the steering wheel and the car drove into a short seep lane, beside a small village green, much smaller than the one they had at home. In the centre of it was a huge sycamore, with a chunky short trunk and long bare branches. The houses were plastered and painted, and some had thatched roofs. The lane narrowed and straightened and stretched away across a wide, flat valley. On each side were bare hedges: there were no stone walls like at home. Ahead was a small bridge.

Sebastian said, with the air of someone who has been saving up something special to say for hours:

'You know what this river is called?' Nobody said anything, because two of the four other people in the car knew, and two didn't.

'Piddle,' said Sebastian. 'That's why the village is called Tolpuddle. It ought to be called Tolpiddle.' Sebastian seemed to be watching everyone.

'Oooh,' Dulcie said.

They came to the bridge. On each side were rather untidy water meadows and a very small river.

'Doesn't seem to be piddling very hard,' Daddy said. Perdita, who had been trying not to laugh, spluttered.

'I'm going to do some more research,' Sebastian said. 'There's a village called Piddle Hinton and another called Puddletown.'

'I read,' Daddy said, 'that Piddletrenthide was called that because in the Domesday Book, it was assessed as having to pay a tax of thirty hides. But in that case why isn't it called Piddle ten hides?'

'Or Piddle trent peaux?' said Mummy. The lane rose out of the water meadows and they came to a place where it split into three. There were high hedges around them. Mummy stopped the car. 'Now, if you two philologists have quite finished, you might get back to reading the jolly map and telling me which way to go.'

They decided that turning right, along the side of the valley, looked the more promising of the three, and Mummy drove the car along it; the lane got narrower, and there was a wood all around them, and suddenly, on the left was a gateway – at least, there were two stone pillars with rather weathered stone eagles crouched on them, and a drive curving through thick woods of green ornamental trees. Everything seemed to be dripping in the cold damp air. They turned a corner and came out on a wide gravel circle. And there was the house: The Grange. Perdita gazed up at lots of worn stone, tall windows, one wing looking much older than the rest; amazing chimneys. And she thought, what a *good* word 'gazed' is: it said exactly what you were doing.

Mummy pulled the car up outside the arched porch with its huge wooden door, with great iron studs in it. But instead of a group of liveried servants, there was only a tall man sitting on the carved stone wall beside the door. He had, Perdita thought, clearly read the right books, and the Earl of Dorincourt could not have been more suitably dressed. He wore a very worn assortment of the things that elderly countrymen in books always wore: layers of a gilet and checked shirt and waxed jacket, and a flat cap. He didn't have a large white moustache or a gun or a spaniel, but he had a very nice smile. .

'Colonel Hughes,' he said. 'You are most welcome to the Grange. Let me show you around. ' He shook hands with all of them, including Dulcie, who was looking at him as if a two headed dragon had suddenly appeared out of the gravel. 'I'll show you the outside first, and then you won't have to take your things off twice.'

He took them around the side of the house, where the stone walls seemed ancient and weathered, and the windows taller and narrower than at the front of the house. 'This was the first part of the house that was built, the Great Hall,' he said. 'Very old. Probably Elizabethan. In those days, all there was was a hall, and the family lived at one end, and the cows and pigs lived at the other end. Very cosy. If smelly.' Perdita was beginning to like him a lot. 'It's now the dining room,' he went on; 'and this is an interesting thing. That's the back of the fireplace.' There was a huge pile of logs and a couple of very large and long branches leaning against the wall. The chimney went up the wall of the house, narrowing every metre or so with a series of steps until it came to the slope of the roof, and then climbed on its own, apparently into the sky. There were tall chimneys, and even some battlements. 'That shows the age of the house,' the Colonel said. 'In the sixteenth century you had to get permission from the King to have battlements!'

He looked down and gestured towards the big branches. 'There's your Yule logs,' he said, 'if you want to burn them on Christmas Day.' Perdita was trying to imagine how big the fireplace would have to be to cope with logs that big, and wondering why they were on the other side of the wall from the fireplace. The Colonel caught her expression. 'I know what you're thinking,' he said, 'but there's something very special here.' He bent down and pointed, and set in the wall was an iron door, almost a metre square. 'You open that,' he said, 'and push the Yule log in, and it burns in the fireplace, when it's burned down a bit, you push it in a bit further. In the old days they used whole bales of old straw.'

And then they were at the front of the house,

Perdita knew that in some books, when you saw something that was really exciting, you were supposed to clap your hands. She had never, until this moment, felt remotely like doing that, so it was rather a pity that her hands were in her pockets (because it was so damp and cold) and so she couldn't clap them. But she suddenly knew how Cedric Erroll must have felt, looking out from Dorincourt Castle.

Along the back of the house – or was it the front? – there was a wide stone terrace, with a wooden frame running around it with trailing withered wintered wisteria. Then there were steps down onto a huge, endless flat lawn, ringed by woods, and at the far end, behind a post-and-rail fence, what looked like a lake.

The Colonel was clearly almost as pleased as Perdita. 'There's an adventure trail in the woods,' he said, 'down by the old mill- but that's just a ruin. And the tennis courts are over there,' he waved an arm, 'although it's a bit cold and wet for that. I'm afraid the swimming pool is covered for the winter – it just gets full of leaves.'

He stepped down onto the lawn, and they all followed, and Dulcie, like a puppy that's been cooped up in a car for too long, went charging off across it, but after a hundred metres or so she suddenly stopped. They caught up with her and saw that she was standing on the edge of the lawn: there was a sudden drop, more than a metre deep, and then the lawns ran on towards the ponds. 'It's called a ha-ha,' the Colonel said. 'It's a sort of upside down fence. You can't see it from the house at all, but it was there to keep cows from getting on to the lawn. We think it might have originally been part of a moat.'

'Why is it called a ha-ha?' Perdita began to say, and then thought she knew, and she remembered a story in which the same thing was called a 'dik'.

'Are those lakes part of the grounds?' Daddy said.

'Yes,' the Colonel said. 'They're not lakes, they're old carp ponds – and originally they were the mill ponds.. They used to be very famous, but they've been rather neglected. I've never been much of a fisherman myself. But I'm told they're full of fish, and you're more than welcome to have a go at them. Sometimes visitors catch some, but mostly they're not fishermen: families use this a s abase to go to the seaside, so the fish are left in peace.' He inclined his head slightly. 'The local lads come and fish the ponds quite a lot. I think they think they're poaching, which makes it more fun, but I don't really mind: it's probably better to keep the fish numbers down. There's certainly some carp; probably a giant pike or two. And perch and bream. There are rods in the house, and there is a dinghy – but it's out of the water at the moment. The oars are in the barn if you need them.'

They walked along the edge of the ha-ha, and Perdita was thinking about a giant pike and how you might have to pull it to the side of the lake and then it would get tangled in the reeds and somebody would have to get into the reeds and maybe fall on it. She decided that she was confusing two stories, and immediately found herself in another one: they had walked along the edge of the woods, which were dripping from the mist, and had come to a high wall. Unlike the house, this wall was built of red bricks, but very old red bricks, with lichen covering them in patches.

There was an open doorway, with dark green ivy growing around it, and Perdita looked around involuntarily for a robin. The walls ran right round the garden, and there were wintry patches of vegetables, and some glass houses with streaks of white paint on the glass.

The Colonel ushered them through the doorway.

'And this is the old kitchen garden – although there's nothing much doing here of course. There's some leeks and brassicas and there's the potato clamp. You're welcome to anything you can find.' He pointed to a long pile of earth with straw sticking out of it. Sebastian had a very Sebastian look on his face, so the Colonel said, 'You take the potatoes from this end, and then clamp it up again. There are layers of straw, and they keep the potatoes fresh.' He considered this for a moment. 'Amazing, really.'

They walked on, past some cucumber frames, Perdita thinking that that you'd have to be a pretty heavy rabbit to break one of those, and then realised that she had no idea how heavy a rabbit might be, and they went out of another door on the far side of the garden.

This was the stable yard, and there were two empty stables. The Colonel seemed to be very interested in what Perdita and Sebastian and Dulcie might be interested in. 'There's a hayloft,' he said cheerfully, 'and a trapdoor or two.' He smiled. 'Normally I'd say don't play in there because the farmer is a bit fussy about having his bales messed around with, but it's almost empty, and the hay's pretty old. Nothing but a few rats.'

Dulcie, who had never quite recovered from 'The Roly-Poly Pudding', said, 'Eugh,' and the Colonel said, 'Nothing to be afraid of. Rats don't eat little girls. Unless they're very hungry, of course.'

'But how do you tell if they're very hungry?' Dulcie said.

'Because they eat you,' Sebastian said. 'But I suppose that's a bit late by then.'

They passed an open cart shed, with old kitchen cupboards ranged along the back. 'There's lots of old tools in there,' the Colonel said: 'saws and spanners and all that. Feel free – but if you need anything fixing, don't worry: just ring me and I'll get the local handyman to come over.'

In the middle of the floor was an orange machine with an engine attached.

'What's that?' Sebastian said.

'It's a log splitter,' Daddy said, so enthusiastically that Mummy looked at him suspiciously.

'It's great fun,' the Colonel said. 'You start it up, put a log on here,' he patted the long orange bar, 'and this spear-thing comes out and the log splits. Please use it – we've left you a supply of logs – and you don't need to replenish it – but we always need more! But don't try to use the old circular saw: that's been out of action for years.' Perdita looked around to see what a circular saw looked like, but the Colonel was already leading them through the outbuildings and round to the gravel drive and the porch.

'I live in the village now, just by the Church, the other side from the Manor. Just a little cottage.'

'Were you brought up here?' Mummy asked

'Yes. And I brought all my children up here, too. All grown and flown, as they say.' He paused. 'But they've left a nice atmosphere behind.'

'Ghosts?' said Perdita, thinking of old houses (in books) where the children had never really gone away.

'Nothing so exciting,' the Colonel said. 'But it's always been a very happy house. Come in and see!'

Chapter 2

In Which there is a Telephone, a Spod, a
Long Alley, and a Small Railway

Perdita enjoyed the next ten minutes in the same way as she enjoyed the first ten minutes in a bookshop. There was so much to read, so many possibilities, and all you could see were the front covers. You could read everything in detail later.

There was a porch, but a porch you could have parked the car in, with logs stacked as high as her head on one side of the doorway. On the other there were rows of hooks and benches and boxes for hanging outdoor clothes and stowing boots. Then there was a stone-flagged hallway with a wide sweep of stone stairs. There were white fairy lights twinkling on the stone banisters. The only furniture was a wooden chair beside an alcove in the wall, which contained an old black telephone. The Colonel paused as they walked by it. 'That's the old house phone,' he said. 'Of course, it isn't connected any more, but we just keep it because…' He stopped, and seemed to remember something. 'Well, it's picturesque.' Then he shook his head and led them through the first door off the hallway, and into the dining room. It had a long black table with twenty-four seats around it (Sebastian, naturally, counted). The massive fireplace, with the iron panel at the back of the grate, for pushing the Yule log through had, rather disappointingly, an electric fire in the middle of it. There were low, empty, glass-fronted cabinets all around, and the whole room had the air of not being loved much, Perdita thought.

Sebastian said: 'Are there any secret passages?'

'Sadly, I don't think so,' the Colonel said. 'My sisters and I once tapped every panel and every brick in the house, but we didn't find anything. But that doesn't mean there aren't any. After all, they were made to be secret.'

The next room, on the corner of the house, was the living room: there were two big sofas, and armchairs, and a more normal sized fireplace with a fire burning, and the sort of fireguard that Granny had at her house, which was great when you were little for playing tigers in when there wasn't a fire. There were small black boxes, each with a padded lid, on each side of the fire, which the Colonel said had belonged to his two sisters when they were little, and which they sat on by the fire, and he'd always been very jealous because he never had one (there being only two sides to a fire). There was a Christmas tree with some tinsel and some very old-looking glass baubles. It was not much bigger than the one at home, but as there was a rule for this holiday that nobody could have more than two presents to put under it – which also meant that there was something to look forward to at home after the holiday – it was probably big enough. There were French windows looking out onto the darkening lawn, and table lamps, and a black grand piano. Daddy reached out and tapped out a few notes.

'Do you play?', said the Colonel politely.

'A little,' Daddy said.

They went back into the hall, and into the next room. 'And this is the library,' the Colonel said. Sebastian stopped so suddenly in the doorway that Perdita bumped into him. It really was a library: there were bookshelves up to the ceiling. True, the upper shelves were empty, and the lower shelves had the sort of paperbacks and DVDs that there had been at all the other holiday houses Perdita had ever been to. But in between there were real books. There was an encyclopedia of about fifty blue-and-gold uniform volumes, which, like all encyclopedias, looked as if it had never been opened. There were guidebooks and maps, and books on fishing on the side tables, and magazines on the rag rug on the floor. There were very big very bulging sofas, and on each side of the fireplace (a smaller fireplace, but still a fireplace, with a log fire burning, and a small and curved fireguard) two chairs with great wing backs that you could hide in to read.

Sebastian looked at Perdita with a slow smile.

They went along the hall and into the *next* room, and Perdita could not but think that the rooms they had seen so far, put together, were bigger than their whole house at home,

'This the family room,' the Colonel, said. 'Playroom or whatever.' There was another fire and tiger-cage fireguard, a trestle table, boxes of board games stacked in a corner and a bookcase with children's books, and another sofa and two window seats in the tall windows that looked out onto the terrace. There was plenty of room for playing in, which Dulcie immediately demonstrated by bouncing off the sofas and the window seats. Mummy made a sort of discouraging gesture, but the Colonel seemed entirely pleased. He had obviously taken to Dulcie, but then, Dulcie had that effect on all known grown-ups. Sebastian had an effect on grown-ups as well, although it was of a rather different kind.

And then there was *another* room, rather narrower than the previous ones. This had a fireplace, but no fire, and some rather stern leather high-backed chairs. But one wall was entirely made of built-in cupboards, rather knocked-about wooden ones. 'This room has had several lives,' the Colonel said. 'Smoking room' – he glanced at Perdita – 'that was where the gentlemen went to smoke after dinner – and it was also the gun room. These were gun racks, but we don't do that any more – never had the taste for it – my father was always rather ashamed of me. I've always been more for sailing. Do you sail?'

He addressed this to Perdita, who said, immediately. 'Only a little. But I've read a lot about it in books.'

'That's what I do in the summer,' the Colonel said. He opened one of the cupboards. 'And this is where we keep things like cricket bats and tennis racquets and fishing tackle.'

There were half a dozen fishing rods of different lengths and thicknesses with boxes of floats, and reels and hooks and some nets. Sebastian was looking at a huge rod which was too long to fit in the cupboard and was leaning against the wall.

'That's a spod rod,' the Colonel said, cheerfully.

'The ponds are full of spods, obviously,' Daddy said.

The Colonel looked at him, Perdita thought, a little speculatively, to see if he was joking, and Daddy adjusted his expression to show that he was, and the Colonel smiled and said that he thought there were some spods in the bottom of the cupboard that they could use, if they wanted to, and they went back into the corridor.

They were now behind the sweeping stone staircase, and there was a green baize door.

'So that's the main house,' the Colonel said: 'now for the servants' quarters.' He pushed the door open, and it moved, Perdita thought, with a green baize sound: a sort of swoosh. The corridor continued. 'That's the Butler's Pantry,' the Colonel said, indicating a door on the left; 'that's now a cloakrooms and loo – and this is another pantry where we keep all the cutlery and glasses.' He began to talk about breakages and Perdita wondered about the house maids and the parlour maids and the between maids – the tweenies – and all the other maids who once dashed up and down the corridors and carried hot water upstairs to the bathrooms and carried it all down again when it was all dirty and cold.

And then they were going into the kitchen. Perdita was the last in line, and she stopped before she followed them, and closed her eyes, and thought of her favourite book-kitchen. She could almost repeat the description in her head:

> … and at once they found themselves in all the glow and warmth of a large fire-lit kitchen.
> The floor was well-worn red brick, and on the wide hearth burnt a fire of logs, between two attractive chimney corners tucked away in the wall, well out of any suspicion of draught. A couple of high-backed settles, facing each other on either side of the fire,

gave further sitting accommodations for the sociably disposed. In the middle of the room stood a long table of plain boards placed on trestles, with benches down each side. At one end of it, where an arm-chair stood pushed back, were spread the remains of the Badger's plain but ample supper. Rows of spotless plates winked from the shelves of the dresser at the far end of the room, and from the rafters overhead hung hams, bundles of dried herbs, nets of onions, and baskets of eggs. It seemed a place where heroes could fitly feast after victory, where weary harvesters could line up in scores along the table and keep their Harvest Home with mirth and song, or where two or three friends of simple tastes could sit about as they pleased and eat and smoke and talk in comfort and contentment. The ruddy brick floor smiled up at the smoky ceiling; the oaken settles, shiny with long wear, exchanged cheerful glances with each other; plates on the dresser grinned at pots on the shelf, and the merry firelight flickered and played over everything without distinction.

Then she opened her eyes and stepped into the real kitchen.

It didn't have a ruddy brick floor smiling up at the smoky ceiling, but apart from that she could have clapped her hands in delight. In fact, as her hands were now warm and not in her pockets, she decided that would be a very good idea, so she clapped them.

The kitchen was bright – although the lights were rather cold – and the modern units around the walls were like any other kitchen units she had ever seen –

or not really seen because, apart from when they had a new cooker and Daddy had knocked the old kitchen cupboards to bits with a hammer she had never really taken any notice of the kitchen cupboards.

But most of all, it was *huge*. It was bigger than the whole downstairs of her house at home, kitchen, hall and living room combined, but it was a nice huge. It had big windows that looked out onto the gravel drive and these threw their grey light over a long table in the centre and cupboards and worktops all around the walls. There was a huge blue AGA cooker, just like Granny's except bigger, on one side, and another huge normal type gas cooker on the other, just like Mummy and Daddy's except bigger. There weren't any hams hanging from the ceiling, but it was a place for feasting if ever she had seen one.

'Now, through here is the games room,' the Colonel said, and led them out through the far door of the kitchen. This opened into a small hallway (with more cupboards) and a back door out onto the gravel drive, and back stairs – things that Perdita had only ever read about – which went up and down, and they went down them, clattering on the bare wood. The Colonel switched on lights with light switches that were on the ends of long square plastic tubes, attached to the bare stone walls, and they came out in a half-cellar, which was, the Colonel said, because it wasn't quite underground – it had narrow horizontal windows at the top of the walls. But it smelt like a cellar despite being a games room with a table-tennis table and a bulky table with a green baize top and coloured shiny balls sitting on it (Perdita had no idea what this was), and there was a dartboard, and along one side, a wooden skittle alley, with nine pins.

'Those are long-alley skittles,' the Colonel said, and Perdita though that this was, so far, the feature of the house of which he was proudest. 'They're dying out these days, but a lot of fun.' He patted the lid of an old trunk. 'That where we keep the darts and spare bats and balls and things. I think we have enough table-tennis balls, although people do tend to tread on them.'

There was a low door at the far end of the room, and the Colonel pushed it open, and a strong smell of old apples rolled out. It was rather like the cellar at the farm near Perdita's house, but you could tell by the shadows that it went on a long way.

'It's just the boiler room now,' the Colonel said, 'but it's quite safe. You can't get lost or fall into anything: we've had children playing here for years and we haven't lost anyone yet.' He looked at Perdita. 'I don't think there are any secret passages. Still, if you find one, let me know.'

And then it was a tour of the bedrooms, which sounded as though it was going to be very boring, and turned out to be even better than what they had seen so far. They went back through the kitchen and through the baize door into the hall and up the stone curving stairs. At the top, a tall ornate window looked over the drive where their car was sitting rather forlornly in the drizzly afternoon.

The landing, which was lined with low bookshelves, mostly, Perdita noted, full of books of history but with occasional patches of children's books, turned into a corridor which had bedrooms with bathrooms attached, and bedrooms without bathrooms, and bathrooms without bedrooms, and doors between some of them, and all excellent, as Dulcie demonstrated, for running in and out of. And when they got to the end of the corridor there were the back stairs coming up from the cellar and the kitchen, and going on up to a dark doorway.

The Colonel trotted up the short flight, pushed open the door, and clicked a light switch. Perdita decided that she had run out of claps and other expressions of delight, and simply looked in delighted silence.

'These used to be the servants' bedrooms, but now it's just attics,' the Colonel said, and even in that second Perdita thought that 'just' was exactly the wrong word. 'Nothing up there much,' the Colonel went on, airily. 'Empty now, But there is,' he said, as if it were a matter of no importance, 'an old model railway. Several visitors have tried to make it work, but I don't think anyone's managed it. And there's an old doll's house, and a box full of dressing-up clothes that belonged to my sisters, if you like that sort of thing. So you're welcome to play here too, but if you do, just one thing – can you stick to the planking to walk on. Don't want anyone falling through the ceilings.'

He went off downstairs with Mummy and Daddy, Dulcie bouncing ahead of them, and Perdita and Sebastian silently waited until they were down in the kitchen and then they tiptoed, because that seemed the thing that you had to do, into the attic. There was a dim light from a round window at the far end – the attic ran the whole length of the wing of the house – and light seemed to leak in here and there under the eaves and round the frames of the old dormer windows, some of which had been boarded up, and some of which were so thickly covered with lichen and mould and dirt that they may as well have been. And there were shapes that might have been boxes with toy soldiers that could come alive and have battles, or that might have been dolls' houses with talking dolls who were hundreds of years old, and there seemed to be a long narrow table running down one side, which might or might not have a model railway on it. Perdita and Sebastian didn't look at eachother, but quietly closed the attic door and went down to the kitchen.

Chapter 3

In Which They Settle in and Learn a Lot about Birds

After the Colonel had gone, and they had brought everything in from the car, and put the bags of food in the kitchen, they took everything else upstairs and stood on the landing.

Daddy said: 'OK. We're here first so we can have the pick of the rooms. We'll put Granny and Grandprof right at the end so they're away from the loudest cousins, but next to Aunty Fee and Uncle Zac and the babies in case Granny wants to play babies. Aunty Cass and Uncle Mike and Jake and Josie and Max can have the middle rooms. Aunty Rill can have the room over the dining room, in the old wing. If there are any ghosts, Rill's just the person to deal with them.' He caught Sebastian looking at him seriously. 'But there aren't any ghosts, and Aunty Rill will go to bed late and lie in for most of the morning, so even if there were, which there aren't, they wouldn't have much time to do haunting.'

Mummy opened the door on the corner of the landing, directly above the living room. 'And this is going to be our room.' It was a very big corner bedroom which had windows looking out over the side and the front of the house. It was so big that there was a three piece suite in it as well as a bed, and there was a door into a big bathroom, and another door out of the bathroom into the next bedroom and that was Perdita's and Sebastian's and Dulcie's room and it had three beds and big windows looking over the lawn.

While Dulcie was testing each bed to see which one she liked best, or, at least, which had the most bounce, Sebastian was inspecting the bathroom doors, both of which had sliding bolts on both sides.

'That,' Mummy said, 'is so that if people want privacy when they're on the loo or in the bath, they lock both the doors from the inside.' She thought about this briefly. 'But don't. If you forget to unlock them Daddy and I won't be able to get in.'

'You can come round through the corridor,' said Sebastian.

'Exactly,' Daddy said.

They had lunch in the kitchen, sitting around the big table and eating toasted cheese sandwiches, and then they sat around the fire in the library, and Mummy put some more logs on, so that the white ash at the edges glowed, and she read the latest episode of *A Christmas Carol*.

Daddy went and played the piano in the living room, and left the door open so that they could hear carols and tunes that circled around the carols. Splatters of rain hit the windows, and Perdita thought that she had never been read to in a better place.

The old miser, Mr Scrooge, had gone home on Christmas Eve to his freezing cold house, and was scared almost to death when his old partner, Jacob Marley, who had been dead for several years, appeared to him, clanking his chains, and showing him a ghostly world:

'Scrooge followed to the window: desperate in his curiosity. He looked out.

'The air was filled with phantoms, wandering hither and thither in restless haste, and moaning as they went. … Many had been personally known to Scrooge in their lives. He had been quite familiar with one old ghost, in a white waistcoat, with a monstrous iron safe attached to its ankle, who cried piteously at being unable to assist a wretched woman with an infant, whom it saw below, upon a door-step. The misery with them all was, clearly, that they sought to interfere, for good, in human matters, and had lost the power for ever.

'Whether these creatures faded into mist, or mist enshrouded them, he could not tell. But they and their spirit voices faded together; and the night became as it had been when he walked home.

'Scrooge closed the window, and examined the door by which the Ghost had entered. It was double-locked, as he had locked it with his own hands, and the bolts were undisturbed. He tried to say "Humbug!" but stopped at the first syllable. And being, from the emotion he had undergone, or the fatigues of the day, or his glimpse of the Invisible World, or the dull conversation of the Ghost, or the lateness of the hour, much in need of repose; went straight to bed, without undressing, and fell asleep upon the instant.

'So let that be a lesson to you,' Mummy said. 'Now. Time for a quick walk, and then we can snuggle in for the rest of the day.'

But the walk didn't last very long, as the wind had risen, and was whipping ice-cold spatterings of rain across the lawns. They went down the steps at the side of the ha-ha and walked as far as the edge of the carp ponds. They were little lakes, really, and the grey water was rippled and splashed by the rain, and on the far side there were reed beds, looking very soggy and bent. There was a jetty, and an upturned boat, and Perdita thought about Dick and Dorothea standing on the side of the lake by themselves.

There was a path along the edge of the pond, and on the right, by the wood, there was a very old wooden sluice gate, with water leaking through it, and lazily dribbling over it. The water formed a small stream, and they followed it, squelching, into the wood, and came to the ruins of a mill, hunched into the dead brambles and undergrowth. It was like the ruins of the mill in the woods by Midsummer Farm, near home, but much smaller and it looked like the kind of place that you could play in without fear of getting drowned.

Above their heads the trees buckled and stirred, and big drops of water plopped onto their hats and hoods. Daddy said that although there was no such thing as bad weather, only incorrect clothing, there was also such a thing as being frozen to death and drowned for no reason, so they went back indoors.

They spent the rest of the afternoon playing with whatever they could find in the playroom, which was rather a lot. They tried old board games and some new board games and Dulcie found a box of wooden train tracks and made a railway all around the playroom, and it got dark outside.

Sebastian was reading from the *Encyclopedia*.

'Did you know?' he began (and Perdita wondered if she should count the number of times that he began sentences like that) 'that the shortest day of the year lasts for seven hours forty-nine minutes and forty-two seconds in London.'

'That sounds about right,' Daddy said. He was pulling the long cords beside the curtains, and they swished together smoothly. 'I've always been scared of doing that,' he said. 'When I was little I did it at Great Granny's house and all the curtains fell down on my head.'

'But do you *know*,' Sebastian went on, as if he hadn't been interrupted, 'that that is more than nine hours shorter than the June solstice. I mean, *nine* hours.'

Perdita, who had been deep in *Winter Holiday*, looked up from wondering what it would be like to have snow, because she could hardly remember what it was like, and thought about that. Could it really mean that in the summer they had had a whole nine more hours every day to play with. What *did* they do with them?

She went back to her book and had got to the part where they were in the *Fram* eating all of Captain Flint's stores when Mummy brought in a big tea tray (and then went back to the kitchen for another one) and laid everything out on the hearthrug – because, she said, the kitchen was really too big and bleak, when there were only the five of them.

'We should be having a chocolate Yule log and spiced mulled wine,' she said. 'So I've got a chocolate Yule log and gingerbread, which is also traditional for some obscure reason, and some fruit punch. And we can pretend that the fire is a bonfire, and I've got a piece of holly instead of a holly wreath, and we could do some dancing after tea.'

'Those are all the things that they used to do for the Saturnalia,' Daddy said.

Sebastian said, 'Doesn't Saturnalia mean that everything is backwards and upside down. So that Dulcie would be in charge, and we can do what we like.'

'Even the old Gods hadn't thought of anything as mad as that,' Mummy said.

They ate their Saturnalian Solstice tea – and there was real food as well – boiled eggs and dippy bread fingers and jam sandwiches and oranges. The big house was quiet all around them, and outside, the evening rained. Afterwards, they helped to clear up and take everything back to the kitchen, which, as Mummy said, was rather bright and if not exactly cold, rather kitcheny.

And then it was bath time. Sebastian and Dulcie wanted to try out all of the nine baths, and they ended up compromising on two – as Daddy said, nobody was looking. And then they went back into the library and Daddy put five more logs on the fire and it shifted and blazed up and crackled and did all the things that fires should do. And Perdita, curled up on the sofa next to Mummy (Dulcie was on Mummy's lap), decided that as long as she didn't look round, whatever was outside the light from the table lamps and the fire would keep itself to itself.

Daddy sat on the rug with Sebastian and an old book.

'Seeing as that was the shortest day,' he said, 'and the Winter Solstice an' all, I've been looking for a winter solstice story.'

'Is it all about ghosts?' said Sebastian.

'No,' Daddy said. 'I'm not having ghost stories in this house. Don't want to frighten myself. No, this is an odd story – it's all about a solstice tradition that's a Christmas tradition, too.

'You know we were saying earlier about Saturnalia, when masters became servants and servants became masters for a week. Well, in the long ago times, the animals did that too, so for a week the foxes had to serve the rabbits, and the wolves had to be nice to the sheep, and the dogs had to be nice to the cats, and the cats had to be nice to the mice. Of course, the trouble was, when it came to the stroke of midnight on the Saturday night, everything changed back to normal, and there was a sudden rush as the foxes tried to eat the rabbits and the rabbits tried to get down into their burrows, and the cats started pouncing on the mice and the dogs started chasing the cats, and it was all very lively.

'Now the only creatures who didn't join in with any of this were the birds. In those days, all the birds were equal. It didn't matter if they were big or small, or fast or slow, or had wide wings or little flippers, they were all, they said, part of the family of birds, and they rather looked down (literally) on the other animals, and thought they were silly to have a pecking order – although of course at that time the birds didn't have a pecking order.'

'And so everything was peaceful in the world of the birds, and on the shortest day of the year, like today, the birds watched – with open beaks – the humans and the animals doing strange Saturnalian things. They thought this was very silly and they all shook their heads and flew away to their nests.

'But there was one bird, the peacock, who had been watching this as well, and he thought that it would be rather nice to be a King and have everyone bow down to you, and you could be boss. And he looked at his reflection in the lake, and thought, "I am the most handsome of all the birds, so I should be King." So he called his strange call, and all the birds few up to see what he was shouting about, and he strutted along the top of the wall – just outside here.

'When they were all settled in front of him, he said "I think it is time that we birds became wise, like the humans and animals, and had a King who is more important than any other bird. And as I'm by far the best looking of you all," – he stretched out his great fan tail with all its rainbow of colours, "it's obvious that I should be King!"

'Now, as you can imagine, there was a lot of clucking ands squawking and whistling about this.

'And then the Peregrine Falcon flew down to the wall (he had been perched on a ledge near the roof) and he said, through his sharp, curved beak: "That is nonsense. I should be King, because I'm the fastest bird in the world, and everyone is afraid of me!"

'There was a silence, because this was true, but then the Duck spoke up from the ponds, and said, "That's all very well, but you may be fast, but that's all. We ducks can fly, and walk, and swim, and dive in the water, so we are much cleverer than you, so we should be the Royal family. And as for everyone being afraid of you, everyone *likes* us, and that is a much better reason for being a King."

'And then the Crows started to chatter from where they sat on the branches of the bare trees over there by the ponds. "That may be so," they said, "but look at us – and listen to us. There are hundreds of us and we are strong and we have black beaks and black feathers and we are louder and fiercer than any other birds. You may be fast, Falcon, and you may be nice, Duck, but together we can fight anybody, and if anybody objects, we can shout louder!" and all the Crows cawed loudly, and the Peacock had to scream a lot to make them calm down.

'But then a low, hooting noise came from the wood. It was the Owl, and the Owl said: "This is all very well, but if any of you were chosen to be King, you would only be King of the Day. When night comes you all go to your nests, but that is when I come into my Kingdom. I am King of the Night, and all night creatures are afraid of me."

'So all the birds were talking at once and nobody knew who to choose. And then there was a sudden silence, as a great shadow fell on all the birds and out of the sky flapped the huge Golden Eagle, and it settled next to the Peacock, and made him look like a sparrow.

'And the Eagle opened its great beak, and said, "I am the strongest and largest of all the birds, and I can fly higher than any of you, and so I should be King!"

'And the Peacock, who could hardly fly at all, was much put out by this, and he thought the Eagle was getting too big for his perch, so he said, "Are you sure of that, Lord Eagle? Are you sure that you can fly higher than any other bird?"

'And the Eagle clicked his beak angrily and said, "I shall prove it to you. Who will challenge me? Anyone who can fly higher than me can be King, but if I fly the highest – as I am certainly going to do – all birds must bow down to me."

'Well, none of the birds liked this very much, so they all decided to challenge the Golden Eagle, and they all took off at once. But the chickens and the peacock soon flopped back down to the ground, and the sparrows and the robins tried hard, but their little wings got tired very quickly. Even the skylarks could not fly as high as the Eagle. For a while the Peregrine Falcon kept up with the Eagle, but his wings were not as wide or as strong, and the Eagle climbed higher and higher, until he seemed to be the only bird in the sky, and when he had got as high as ever he could, and could fly not an inch higher, he rested on the air, and called down, "Now, who is King of all the Birds?" – and a little voice said, "I am," and the Wren, the tiniest of birds, who had been hiding among the Eagle's golden feathers, just behind his head, flew out and flew even higher, and the air was so thin that it wouldn't bear the weight of the Eagle and the Eagle couldn't catch the Wren!

'And so that is why the Wren is King of all the Birds – but it is also why it's very difficult to find a Wren – because the Eagle was very angry and the Wren has been hiding from it ever since.'

They looked at the fire. 'Clever Wren,' said Dulcie.

'But what's it got to do with Christmas?' Sebastian said.

'Well,' Daddy said, 'in some places, there is a tradition of Wren Hunting at Christmas – actually, Boxing Day is known as the Day of the Wren in some places. People seem to think that if you're having the King of Heaven, you should have the King of the Birds too, so they have Wren Boys who catch Wrens – don't ask me how – and put them in a little house – a Wren House – which has painted doors and windows on it, and they parade it around the village, or they have a pretend wren and put it on top of a pole. There's even a song:

"The wren, the wren, the king of all birds
St Stephen's Day was caught in the furze.
Her clothes were all torn,
Her shoes were all worn,
Up with the kettle and down with the pan
Give us a penny to bury the wran.
If you haven't a penny a halfpenny will do
If you haven't a halfpenny
God bless you!".'

And then it was bedtime.

'We've decided,' Mummy said, 'that we'll all go to bed at the same time. It doesn't seem fair to put old Dulcie to bed on her own when it's about three miles from there to here.' Perdita looked at her and wondered whether it was just Dulcie she was thinking about. After all, instead of the cosy three rooms upstairs in her house at home that she usually went to sleep in, or next to, here there were great empty unoccupied spaces, cellars and attics and bedrooms where nobody was, nobody seeing them, and if you don't see places, do they exist? Or were spirits like old Jacob Marley's clanking around out there and up and down the corridors? Perhaps Mummy would like to have Dulcie around just as much as Dulcie would like to have Mummy around.

Daddy tided the fire and the hearth, and they went out into the hallway, which suddenly seemed to be rather cold and echoing. Perdita thought that they really should have been carrying candles or oil lamps, and even with the electric lights the stairway seemed to be built on shadows.

When they were all in bed, and Dulcie's light was out, and she and Sebastian were reading by the glow of their bedside lights, she could see into the bathroom, the door being ajar slightly, and across the bathroom into Mummy and Daddy's room. Their bedside lights were on too, so Mummy and Daddy would be reading too, and Perdita could not help feeling that they were in a sort of warm and light cocoon. On the other side of her bedroom door was the landing, and the landing was dark, and nothing moved on the stairs or in the corridor, or down in the cellar. She hoped.

Sebastian suddenly got up and went to tell Mummy and Daddy that it wasn't just recently that people had decided to change the name of the nearby villages from Piddle to Puddle, because Puddletown was still called Piddletown on the maps in the 1950s but on John Speed's map of 1610 it was already called Puddletown, and was politely asked to go back to bed and to start to go to sleep.

Perdita had just finished reading *The Secret Garden* again, and was wondering whether they'd find a swing in the walled kitchen garden, when Mummy and Daddy came quietly into the bedroom with an envelope and sat down on her bed. Dulcie was gently snoring.

'Bet time,' Daddy said, and opened the envelope. There was a sheet of paper with the list of guesses as to how many times Dulcie would ask 'Are we nearly there?' in the car on their way to Tolpuddle. Daddy had said fifty, Mummy had said twenty, Perdita had said fifteen, but Sebastian was closest with twelve, as it was actually only eleven times. Daddy said that it *seemed* like fifty times, so he should win. The prize was that next time Grandprof dispensed a round of Jelly Babies, Sebastian would have two. And Dulcie would get an extra one because she couldn't join in. And then Daddy said that that wasn't really fair on Perdita, and Mummy said never mind Perdita, what about her, so they decided that they would all have two Jelly Babies, but that Sebastian could have an extra one.

By common consent, although they never had a nightlight at home, it was agreed that they would leave on the little light that was over the wash basin ('wash-hand basin,' said Sebastian) in the bathroom, just in case anyone woke up and wandered.

This meant, Perdita found, that there was enough light to show that the ceiling above her bed was rather saggy, and had lots of cracks and lines on it which you could if you liked turn into all sorts of animals which might, possibly, come to eat you up in the night. But she also found that one of them looked rather like a map of Africa, and she was just wondering if she could see where Sri Lanka was, when it was morning.

23 DECEMBER

Chapter 4

In Which Baking Begins and there are Lots of Cousins and Stairs

When Perdita woke up, there was grey light around the curtains; Dulcie was snuffling in her bed, with her big white lamb sharing her pillow, and Sebastian's bed was empty, with the duvet half on the floor. Perdita slipped out of bed and went to the bathroom. She wondered whether to lock one or other or either of the doors while she went to the loo, but decided that it was very complicated and anyway it didn't matter if anyone saw you on the loo. As Granny said, everybody did it so it wasn't going to be a surprise.

When she'd finished, she looked into Mummy and Daddy's bedroom, which did not contain a Mummy or a Daddy, and she went back into her bedroom, wondering whether to go downstairs without waking Dulcie. But she had a sudden vision of what might happen if Dulcie woke up, found herself in a totally strange bedroom and panicked, so she went over to the curtains and found the cord and pulled it and Dulcie woke up. Outside it was grey, but there were signs of sunshine and a distant blue sky, so she caught Dulcie, who was halfway across the landing, and put her dressing gown and slippers on for her, and put her own on and they went down the wide stone staircase, very regally, with Dulcie being a page-girl and holding up the back of Perdita's dressing gown.

Mummy and Daddy and Sebastian were sitting at the kitchen table, and Mummy was saying things about how odd the AGA was that would not have pleased Granny.

Sebastian had one of the books from the library open beside his bowl of porridge: 'This is about the haunted manor up the river, called Athelhampton and in the Domesday Book it was called Pidele. And the family was called de Pidyle.' He spelt it out.

'Quite a long way from piddle, then,' Daddy said.

'Once a piddle always a piddle', Mummy said.

They ate breakfast, and afterwards Perdita thought that that must have been the last calm, and peaceful, and normal moment in the whole holiday.

They had just got properly dressed when everyone started to arrive, and Perdita felt that she had been thrown into a book called *Fifteen Cousins at Mayhem Manor*. She and Sebastian had started to walk down the drive to meet whoever came first when Granny and Grandprof arrived in Grandprof's big old red estate car, and they climbed into the back seat and sat with the turkey, which was in large box, between them, and rode back to the house in grand style.

Then they had just finished carrying Granny and Grandprof's bags up to their room, and had shown Granny the kitchen, where she went and stroked the AGA, when there was much hooting outside the front door and Aunty Cass and Uncle Mike and Jake and Josie and Max, the fastest toddler in the world, were upon them.

Aunty Cass was rather like Granny: around her there was always an air of buzzing and doing, and she whirled by and kissed everybody and disappeared along the hallway and into the kitchen with bags and packages and Max under one arm, and Dulcie dancing behind them. (Dulcie was a big fan of Aunty Cass.) She and Granny were, Perdita thought, immediately starting to bake about fifty different kinds of cake. And Jake and Josie fell out of the back of the car and danced around them and there was a lot of energetic hugging and Sebastian and Perdita started to take them up to show them their room and everything else, and had just got to the porch when Uncle Mike's calm voice called them back to take their bags with them. Jake had a very neat bag and Josie had several carrier bags with bits of dolls poking out at all angles. They had nearly got to the porch for a second time when Uncle Mike called them back again, again, very calmly – Uncle Mike did everything very calmly. He was very *very* tall and Perdita thought that he made her think of a very tall pine tree, or a mountain, if you could imagine a tall thin mountain – with clouds around the top, where everything was peaceful, while in the foothills, things – notably Aunty Cass and Jake and Josie and Max were swirling around in continual movement. Now, Uncle Mike calmly made Jake and Josie take their boots and put them in the hall, Then he calmly went on unpacking the car. He waved to Perdita, who was watching this mad back-and-forth going on, and Perdita, who liked him a lot, gave a small wave with the ends of her fingers, and then she was caught up in the mad dash around the house.

First they went up the stairs to the bedrooms, with Jake bounding up the stairs and disappearing into doorways when he didn't know what was on the other side of them, while Josie, who, like Jake and her mother, seemed to have more arms than most people, floundered along behind him, shedding dolls, which Perdita and Sebastian picked up. By the time they arrived at the right bedroom they were carrying most of Josie's things, but, like her brother, Josie was so endlessly cheerful that you couldn't possibly mind doing anything for her.

So then it was exploring everything in the house again. After an hour Jake had nearly fallen out of the attic, and down all available stairs, but always managed to not quite break anything, and trodden on a table-tennis ball, and knocked down all nine pins in the skittle alley with a single ball, and knocked down half the pile of logs in the porch. Josie, who sometimes seemed to have a lack of connection between what her head said, and what her body did, had fallen over everything it was possible to fall over, and apparently bounced. Perdita was feeling somewhat breathless, and she was slightly relieved when Jake and Uncle Mike and Sebastian disappeared into the attic to see whether they could get the railway to work.

She wouldn't have minded watching the railway, but it seemed rather overcrowded in the attic, so she went cheerfully downstairs. In the playroom, Josie and Dulcie were playing dolls. Then there seemed to be a lot happening in the kitchen, where Daddy was making soup and Granny was making bread and Aunty Cass was organising everything and trying to stop Max from climbing up everything and opening all the drawers and cupboards and helpfully emptying them.

Suddenly, the house seemed a lot warmer, as if it was enjoying itself, and as she went from room to room Perdita began to feel as if the house was like the chicken houses on wheels that Grandprof sometimes talked about. The chicken houses had nesting boxes along each side, which the chickens could get to from the inside, but each one had a lid, so you could open them from the outside. That was, Grandprof said, very exciting because when you lifted the lid you might find nothing, or you might find a hen sitting on some eggs and it would squawk and peck at you, or you might find one egg, or several eggs, just lying there waiting to be picked up and put in your basket. Now the house was like that. Look into any room, and you never knew what you would find, and it would always be interesting.

So she went into the library and found, not a chicken, but Grandprof, sitting in one of the big chairs in front of the fire, reading. After all the happy chaos, Grandprof was a very calming person to be with, and she went and sat next to him, and snuggled under his arm. He was reading a very small, square book.

'Look what I found,' Grandprof said. 'It's one of my favourite books. I won it – not this copy – but one almost exactly the same, as a school prize when I was twelve.' He patted the book, 'But can I tell you a secret? I've only ever read the first chapter. Perhaps I'll get time to read a bit more.'

'Perhaps that's the best bit,' Perdita said, 'The first chapter often is the best bit.'

Grandprof nodded. 'It's about an attic,' he said. 'Shall I read it to you?' Grandfathers, Perdita knew, were supposed to smell of tweed and tobacco – whatever they smelt like – just as Grandmothers were supposed to smell of lavender. Perdita had never considered what people smelt like. Grandprof just smelt warm. She said, 'Mmmm,' and Grandprof read:

'They burned the old gun that used to stand in the dark corner up in the garret, close to the stuffed fox that always grinned so fiercely. Perhaps the reason why he seemed in such a ghastly rage was that he did not come by his death fairly. Otherwise his pelt would not have been so perfect. And why else was he put away up there out of sight?—and so magnificent a brush as he had too. But there he stood, and mounted guard over the old flintlock that was so powerful a magnet to us in those days. Though to go up there alone was no slight trial of moral courage after listening to the horrible tales of the carters in the stable, or the old women who used to sit under the hedge in the shade, on an armful of hay, munching their crusts at luncheon time.

The great cavernous place was full of shadows in the brightest summer day; for the light came only through the chinks in the shutters. These were flush with the floor and bolted firmly. The silence was intense, it being so near the roof and so far away from the inhabited parts of the house. Yet there were sometimes strange acoustical effects—as when there came a low tapping at the shutters, enough to make your heart stand still. There was then nothing for it but to dash through the doorway into the empty cheese-room adjoining, which was better lighted. No doubt it was nothing but the labourers knocking the stakes in for the railing round the rickyard, but why did it sound just exactly outside the shutters? When that ceased the staircase creaked, or the pear-tree boughs rustled against the window. The staircase always waited till you had forgotten all about it before the loose worm-eaten planks sprang back to their place.

'Had it not been for the merry whistling of the starlings on the thatch above, it would not have been possible to face the gloom and the teeth of Reynard, ever in the act to snap, and the mystic noises, and the sense of guilt—for the gun was forbidden. Besides which there was the black mouth of the open trapdoor overhead yawning fearfully—a standing terror and temptation; for there was a legend of a pair of pistols thrown up there out of the way—a treasure-trove tempting enough to make us face anything.

'We dragged an ancient linen-press under the trapdoor, and put some boxes on that, and finally a straight-backed oaken chair. One or two of those chairs were split up and helped to do the roasting on the kitchen hearth. So, climbing the pile, we emerged under the rafters, and could see daylight faintly in several places coming through the starlings' holes. One or two bats fluttered to and fro as we groped among the lumber, but no pistols could be discovered; nothing but a cannon-ball, rusty enough and about as big as an orange, which they say was found in the wood.

'In the middle of our expedition there came the well-known whistle, echoing about the chimneys, with which it was the custom to recall us to dinner. How else could you make people hear who might be cutting a knobbed stick in the copse half a mile away or bathing in the lake? We had to jump down with a run; and then came the difficulty; for black dusty cobwebs, the growth of fifty years, clothed us from head to foot. There was no brushing or picking them off, with that loud whistle repeated every two minutes.

'The fact where we had been was patent to all; and so the chairs got burned—but one, which was rickety. After which a story crept out, of a disjointed skeleton lying in a corner under the thatch. Though just a little suspicious that this might be a ruse to frighten us from a second attempt, we yet could not deny the possibility of its being true. Sometimes in the dusk, when I sat reading by the little window in the cheese-room, a skull seemed to peer down the trapdoor.'

'I haven't really been in the attics yet,' Perdita said. 'They were rather crowded.'

'Great things, attics,' Grandprof said. 'They're like the house's memories. All sorts of things get stuffed into them and forgotten, and then suddenly remembered.'

And then there were cheerful shouts and Aunty Fee had arrived with Laura – who was bigger than Max and smaller that Dulcie – and Amelia, the new baby, who lay around a lot, and, Perdita thought, only smiled at people when nobody else was looking. And Uncle Zac, who was the champion reader of stories in a family of champion readers, and who everyone liked to climb on. He said it was just a talent and it was the same with dogs, and it was probably to do with what he smelt like.

More hugging and then it was lunch which was very noisy and Granny and Aunty Cass had both made soups. Perdita tried both of them to be polite, and because Daddy had said that all cooks should be encouraged, however awful. She couldn't tell the soups apart, and they tasted like the soups that Mummy and Daddy made, which always tasted the same whatever they were made of. So she didn't say anything, but ate a kind of cheese that she had never seen before, with some of Granny's new bread, which *was* very nice, and nobody was watching to see how much butter she put on it.

Uncle Zac sat in the corner with Amelia, watching, while Aunty Fee had her lunch, and then Aunty Fee sat in the corner and fed Amelia while Uncle Zac had his lunch (with Josie and Dulcie on his knees).

And after lunch …

Chapter 5

In Which there is Someone in the Woods, and
Sir Roger de Coverley in the House

What happened after lunch was like what happened in the morning except that it happened outside, but Perdita could not help but notice that apart from Amelia – who, being tied to Uncle Zac's front didn't have a choice – she was the only girl not indoors. Uncle Zac and Uncle Mike and Daddy were in charge, and Jake and Sebastian charged about the garden and the woods, and Max divided his time between charging after them and sitting on Uncle Mike's shoulders and being charged.

Perdita, who could charge about with the best of them, nevertheless worried about this slightly. When she had read *Little Women* she thought that Jo was a very good person, but she liked the other sisters and thought that Meg was sensible to have nice clothes and get married if she liked John Brooke. When she read *Swallows and Amazons* her favourite character wasn't Nancy the active leader girl, or Susan the motherly cook, or even Titty, the bookish, thoughtful one. It was Peggy, who could do everything that anyone else could do but didn't make a fuss about it. What girls did and what boys did didn't have to be different.

So, she wasn't particularly interested in fishing, but couldn't see why she shouldn't be, and when they got to the carp ponds, and stood on the little jetty she was just as interested as the others were in whether there were any fish in there, and how one might get them out.

They stood and watched to see if they could see any fish rising, but as Uncle Mike said, any really sensible fish would have its nose in the mud, and Jake if you want to catch fish, it's a good idea not to stamp around quite so much. And Perdita, trying to feel like a fish, thought that sensible fish might be near to the reeds on the far side of the pond, where there wasn't a path and with nobody stamping about. The trouble was that it was difficult to get anywhere near that side of the lake without a boat, and the only one they had was still upside down.

'That's where the spod comes in,' said Uncle Mike, who knew about this sort of thing, and seemed to be reading her mind. 'It's all about ground-baiting,' and Daddy and Uncle Zac nodded wisely, as Daddies and Uncles do.

'We'll try the spod first thing tomorrow,' Uncle Mike said. 'and see how we go. And then we'll get the boat onto the water.'

And then they walked to the sluice, then down into the wood and the mill. There were a lot of plans made about damming the stream beside the old mill, although Perdita could not see quite why you might want to do this. It seemed that it was just fun to build dams. Daddy was looking at the woods.

'This must be very ancient,' he said. 'There's no sign at all of a track or a road. And they must have had one. I wonder what they milled?'

But there was a sort of path that shuffled through the trees and back onto the lawns above the ha-ha, and past the closed up swimming pool, with its gate locked, and its changing hut shuttered, and blue sheets stretched over its empty bottom.

They came in through the front door, and were taking their waterproofs off and shaking water, when Uncle Zac said: 'We're one short. Anyone seen Jake?'

Perdita knew what happened now: everyone would get very worried and tea would be late, and a search party would be about to set off when Jake would walk back into the light of the hallway and say that he'd found a goldmine. In fact, just when Uncle Mike was getting his boots on again, Jake did come back. He'd just followed the stream a bit further down through the woods, where it was rather misty, he said. But there wasn't a track.

'I did see someone in the woods,' he said.

'What sort of someone?' Uncle Mike said, taking his boots off and putting them on the big boot rack.

'Oh, a chap,' Jake said. 'About Uncle Zac's height. And he was wearing a big cape.' Jake, for all his endless energy and tendency to go off in random directions, had a very precise and methodical mind. 'But he had a very strange face. I just caught a glimpse of it.'

Perdita looked at him to see whether he was quoting from the sort of story where you saw strange people in the woods in the moonlight, possibly leading ponies with barrels of brandy. But Jake lived in a different world, where books were things that helped you learn how to make a dam, or mend a model railway, or catch a carp.

But not where you would meet strange people in the woods at dusk.

'I said, "Hi,"' Jake said, 'but he just went on walking.' He dropped his anorak on the floor and then, under Uncle Mike's eye, went back and picked it up and hung it on one of the crowded hooks, and then went back again and took it down and shook it and hung it on an empty hook. Uncle Mike stopped looking at him.

'What did he look like?' said Uncle Zac, unwinding Amelia from the long fabric shawl.

Something in his voice made Perdita look at him. Uncle Zac was clearly more interested in the world that was actually out there than any books.

Jake had obviously almost forgotten about the man. 'He had a funny cheek,' he said. 'Looked like, you know, when Mummy's making pastry, and before she rolls it out it's a ball and you stick your finger in it.'

'A dimple,' Sebastian said.

'A pock mark?' said Daddy. 'That's a word.'

'That's it,' Jake said. 'Like a pirate.'

'No eye patch?' Uncle Zac said.

Jake grinned. 'No, but he did have a scar. Really. Under his right eye.' He went into the hall and along the passage towards the kitchen.

'Probably one of the local lads poaching,' Daddy said. 'Scared off by our howling mob.'

Perdita, with some things to think about, went upstairs to her bathroom and rubbed her hair dry, and then went downstairs. Something was definitely happening in the living room. Uncle Zac and Amelia were on the sofa, Granny and the Mummies were leaning against the walls, Uncle Mike was lying on the floor balancing Max on his feet, and Daddy was marshalling everyone else for carols practice. Perdita took her place next to Jake.

Grandprof was handing out carol sheets, and Daddy sat down at the piano, and they sang 'Away in a manger', 'Hark the Herald', and Granny's favourite, 'Hey, little bull behind the gate'.

'OK,' Daddy said. 'Very good. More tomorrow.' He shuffled the carol sheets and put them neatly on the top of the piano.

Grandprof had settled himself on the sofa with a book, and Granny and the Mummies (and Max) disappeared into the kitchen, and as Grandprof read, the room and everyone in it settled quietly around him.

'"What's up?" inquired the Rat, pausing in his labours.

"I think it must be the field-mice," replied the Mole, with a touch of pride in his manner. "They go round carol-singing regularly at this time of the year. They're quite an institution in these parts. And they never pass me over – they come to Mole End last of all; and I used to give them hot drinks, and supper too sometimes, when I could afford it. It will be like old times to hear them again."

"Let's have a look at them!" cried the Rat, jumping up and running to the door.

It was a pretty sight, and a seasonable one, that met their eyes when they flung the door open. In the fore-court, lit by the dim rays of a horn lantern, some eight or ten little field-mice stood in a semicircle, red worsted comforters round their throats, their fore-paws thrust deep into their pockets, their feet jigging for warmth. With bright beady eyes they glanced shyly at each other, sniggering a little, sniffing and applying coat-sleeves a good deal. As the door opened, one of the elder ones that carried the lantern was just saying, "Now then, one, two, three!" and forthwith their shrill little voices uprose on the air, singing one of the old-time carols that their forefathers composed in fields that were fallow and held by frost, or when snow-bound in chimney corners, and handed down to be sung in the miry street to lamp-lit windows at Yule-time.'

Perdita particularly liked the next bit, and was just relishing the idea of the Mice going shopping in the snow, when there was a heavy crunching in the drive, and everyone except Uncle Zac, who sat placidly by the fire with Amelia. ran to the front door.

There was a large white van, backing up to the kitchen door, so they all ran along the passage in time to see a man in a white coat with an anorak on top of it, coming into the kitchen with a crate.

'What's inside it?' said Josie.

Grandprof laughed. 'There's cold chicken inside it,' he said. 'Coldtonguecoldhamcoldbeefpickledgherkins saladfrenchrollscresssandwichespottedmeatgingerbeer lemonadesodawater.'

Perdita had never seen so much food. Crate after crate was carried in. A crate of potatoes and carrots and parsnips. Another of oranges and nuts and grapes. A whole crate of crisps. And flour and oil, and sausages and bacon and whole trays of eggs, and bottles and bottles of milk. There were cheeses and mustards and packets of bread sauce. And balloons.

'Well there are a lot of us,' said Aunty Cass as if apologetically. 'But at least it arrived before the snow.'

'Is it going to snow?' said Perdita.

'Tomorrow, probably,' Uncle Mike said. ''That's what they say.'

Teatime was now being delayed while all the food was unpacked, and so Uncle Zac was recruited to read more of *A Christmas Carol*. The ghost of Christmas past had taken Scrooge back in time to when he was happy, and when he went to a party thrown by his old master, Mr Fezziwig.

> 'In came a fiddler with a music-book, and went
> up to the lofty desk, and made an orchestra of it,
> and tuned like fifty stomach-aches. In came Mrs.
> Fezziwig, one vast substantial smile. In came the three
> Miss Fezziwigs, beaming and lovable. In came the six
> young followers whose hearts they broke. In came all
> the young men and women employed in the business.
> In came the housemaid, with her cousin, the baker.
> In came the cook, with her brother's particular friend,
> the milkman. In came the boy from over the way, who
> was suspected of not having board enough from his
> master; trying to hide himself behind the girl from
> next door but one, who was proved to have had her
> ears pulled by her mistress. In they all came, one after
> another; some shyly, some boldly, some gracefully,
> some awkwardly, some pushing, some pulling; in they
> all came, anyhow and everyhow.

Away they all went, twenty couple at once; hands half round and back again the other way; down the middle and up again; round and round in various stages of affectionate grouping; old top couple always turning up in the wrong place; new top couple starting off again, as soon as they got there; all top couples at last, and not a bottom one to help them! When this result was brought about, old Fezziwig, clapping his hands to stop the dance, cried out, "Well done!" and the fiddler plunged his hot face into a pot of porter, especially provided for that purpose. But scorning rest, upon his reappearance, he instantly began again, though there were no dancers yet, as if the other fiddler had been carried home, exhausted, on a shutter, and he were a bran-new man resolved to beat him out of sight, or perish.

There were more dances, and there were forfeits, and more dances, and there was cake, and there was negus…' (There was a pause while Sebastian went off to find out what negus was, and reported that it was a drink made of port wine and lemon and sugar and there was a great piece of Cold Roast, and there was a great piece of Cold Boiled, and there were mince pies, and plenty of beer. But the great effect of the evening came after the Roast and Boiled, when the fiddler (an artful dog, mind! The sort of man who knew his business better than you or I could have told it him!) struck up "Sir Roger de Coverley." Then old Fezziwig stood out to dance with Mrs. Fezziwig. Top couple, too; with a good stiff piece of work cut out for them; three or four and twenty pair of partners;

people who were not to be trifled with; people who would dance, and had no notion of walking.

'And then,' said Uncle Zac, as Daddy came into the room to call them to tea, 'Mr Fezziwigg's party danced the Sir Roger de Coverley,' and as Daddy knew all the dances in the world, he sat down at the piano, and Uncle Zac and Uncle Mike moved the chairs back, and when Granny and Aunty Cass came to see where everyone was because the muffins were getting cold they joined in, and Aunty Fee and the baby came and joined in too.

And in the middle of the dance, Perdita felt another hand holding hers, and Aunty Rill had arrived.

Chapter 6

In Which we Learn about Spods, and Martyrs Who Weren't Martyred

Aunty Rill was the Aunty who didn't bring any cousins with her, but bought all the other cousins all the birthday and Christmas presents that they were not *really* supposed to have (Josie's pink flashing Unicorn was still famous) and who had told Perdita that if she ever wanted to run away from home, she could come to live with her. Perdita had never wanted to run away from home, but she had stayed for a night on Aunty Rill's barge (with Sebastian) and they had agreed that if they ever *did* want to run away from home then that was the place they would run to. (Aunty Rill's barge didn't go anywhere, but it was moored in the middle of a big city, and you could watch big boats going by, and their wash made you think that you might be at sea.)

And so by the time they had all showed Aunty Rill where her bedroom was, and all the other bedrooms, and the attic and the cellar, teatime was *very* late. And then bath time was made later by Aunty Rill insisting that they have a Jelly Baby hunt before bath time. It did mean that Aunty Fee and Granny got to bathe Amelia before the mayhem broke out.

'You know,' Mummy said to Perdita, as Perdita jumped out of her bath and went to try one of the other baths, 'bath time is meant to be when everybody calms down for the night.' Perdita just grinned at her and ran down the hallway. Laura was being bathed in one bathroom, loosely supervised by Uncle Zac, and Dulcie decided that she wanted to be bathed in that one, too; and Perdita and Sebastian were having their bath when Jake came and jumped in too, so Sebastian ran along the corridor and jumped in with Josie, and then Aunty Rill filled Granny and Grandprof's bath and started a race to see who could get in and out of all the baths the quickest. Daddy seemed to have disappeared, and Perdita caught a glimpse of Uncle Mike lying on his bed reading a magazine as she ran past his bedroom door.

This went on with much shrieking until there was a wet route along the corridor and in and out of the bathrooms – or, more exactly, until Granny and Mummy came upstairs and put a stop to it.

After that, Perdita wandered back to her bedroom and dried herself and put her pyjamas and dressing gown and slippers on. Things seemed to have gone quiet, and it seemed distinctly odd not to know where everybody was, rather than knowing exactly where everybody was, as happened at home.

She went downstairs.

Jake was having a discussion with Uncle Mike and Sebastian in the smoking room about how to catch carp. Perdita stood in the doorway listening, fascinated. It's amazing how many other worlds there are out there, she thought, not just that you don't think about, but that you *can't* think about.

Jake had looked up catching carp in one of the books in the playroom, and it seemed that the best time to catch them was after three o'clock in the afternoon, although Grandprof argued that the carp really didn't know what time it was, and it would be getting pretty dark by then. But it meant that they would have to bait the swims a couple of hours before,

'Excuse me' Perdita said. 'What does that mean?'

Uncle Mike looked round. 'Baiting the swim,' he said. 'Well, you've seen the ponds out there; they're quite big, and the fish could be anywhere. So you need to attract them to a particular patch of water – called a swim – so that when you start fishing, they're there and ready to bite. So you fill the water with tasty little tit-bits, enough to attract them but small enough so they're still hungry.'

Perdita nodded.

'So, if you're on a canal,' Uncle Mike said, 'you can just throw handfuls of bait – it's called ground bait –'

'That's because it's ground up,' Jake said.

Uncle Mike shook his head. 'No, actually. It's called ground bait because it prepares the ground for real fishing.' He reached into the cupboard and pulled out two bullet-shaped things.

'You see, ideally,' he went on, looking at them carefully, 'you should put ground bait as far away from where you're sitting as possible, because the fish are very sensitive to any vibrations. If the river is wide, you can use a catapult to spray the ground bait. But if it's a really long way to the other side of the lake, like it is here, you use a spod.' He held the thing up. It had black body, with holes along each side. 'So you fill these spods with ground bait and swing them out with a great big long rod and they go for miles.' He pointed to the long rod leaning against the wall. 'You see, the nose of the spod is buoyant so that when it hits the water it turns upside down and spills out the bait. Then you leave it for a bit and all the fish come swarming around. At least, that's the idea. I'll show you tomorrow— but we need to see if we can get everything together first.' Uncle Mike was a methodical man.

Perdita was about to move on to see what else was happening, when Sebastian, who had been reading another book, wanted to know what they thought about the best recipe for baits, which seemed to be tinned sweetcorn and vanilla extract. And they all went off to the kitchen to ask Granny and Aunty Cass whether they had any sweetcorn and vanilla extract. Daddy was cooking at the AGA.

Aunty Cass said, 'You're kidding me.'

And Sebastian said, 'Well, if you haven't got that, how about crumbled Weetabix and garlic. Peanut butter and chicken livers? Hemp seed and squid powder?'

'Just run out,' Aunty Cass said.

'Call this a kitchen,' Daddy said.

'Angel delight and custard powder,' Sebastian said.

'Go and find Grandprof,' Daddy said. 'He's doing tonight's story,' and so they left the recipe for ground bait and drifted into the library, where Grandprof and Josie and Dulcie were already sitting by the fire, reading *Angelina's Christmas*. Uncle Zac and Amelia were in the corner nearest the fire, and Aunty Rill was stretched on the sofa, so they all went and sat on her.

'I'm glad you've come,' Aunty Rill said. 'That Angelina book is soooo sad.'

'I'm not allowed to tell you a ghost story,' Grandprof said, 'so I'm going to tell you some history. This is *real*.

And as we're in Tolpuddle, I'll tell you about the famous martyrs. This is what REALLY happened.'

Daddy wandered into the room, put some more logs on the fire, and faded into the background, which Perdita thought was really rather clever.

'This is two hundred years ago,' Grandprof said, 'and things were very hard then, especially around here, where the land isn't very fertile, and the water meadows in the valley flood a lot.'

'That's why they're called water meadows,' Sebastian said.

'Do you know,' Grandprof said, ignoring him, 'the expression "as different as chalk and cheese"? This is where it comes from. The chalk hills around here are very poor for agriculture, but over towards Bristol, the land is much better and they had lots of cows and lots of milk and made lots of cheese, in Cheddar and Gloucestershire – double Gloucester – so the farmers there were much richer than the farmers here. So that was the difference between chalk and cheese.' Perdita clapped her hands, as this seemed to her to be absolutely brilliant, but she could see that nobody else thought so, so she rather hurriedly put her hands away.

Grandprof went on: 'People lived on tea, bread and potatoes – and every now and then the harvest would fail, and they had hardly anything to eat – and there were some very bad years at the beginning of the 1830s. I read about one man – called James Loveless – and he had three wives, who all died, and nine children, and all but one of them died either at birth or very young. And the saddest thing was that the last three were all called Jenny.'

They thought about that, and Josie said, 'That's very very sad.'

'But what about the martyrs?' Perdita said. She was thinking of the pictures of martyrs that she had seen in some very old books and mostly people who were martyrs had been martyred by having bits cut off them or arrows stuck in them, and other things she didn't like to think about.

'Well, that's it,' said Grandprof. 'Depends what you mean by martyrs. These were pretty happy ones, really. Basically, this was 1833, and some workers in Tolpuddle were protesting at their wages being cut, because the farmers and the land owners wanted to make all the money they could, so the less they paid the workers the more money they kept for themselves.

'So these workers formed a Union and took secret oaths to be brothers and try to get higher wages – and they met under that big sycamore tree in the middle of the village green. You came past it when you drove in.

'Of course the landowners didn't like the idea of paying bigger wages, but as the workers weren't actually doing any harm, like breaking things up, or striking or anything like that they weren't sure how to get rid of them. So the local magistrate dug up an old law that said it was illegal to take secret oaths, and six of them were arrested.

'There was a lot of bad feeling – there was a Methodist Chapel at one end of the village, and a Church at the other – still is, I think – and most of the Union men were Methodists. And the Vicar of the church wasn't a nice man. Apparently, the landowners made a deal with the workers for fair wages, and the Vicar was witness to it – but then the landowners changed their minds, and the Vicar backed them up – and so the six workers were sentenced to seven years transportation to Australia. And the day they were sentenced somebody broke the windows in the Vicarage.'

'But Australia's nice,' Perdita said, with pictures of broad beaches and blue skies and kangaroos in her mind.

'It wasn't then,' Grandprof said. 'It was all snakes and spiders and things that will eat you or poison you. Come to think of it, it still is.'

'They have the most poisonous spiders in the world,' said Sebastian.

'And the most poisonous snakes,' said Jake. '*And* the most poisonous sea snakes.'

Perdita looked at them.

Grandprof went on: 'And getting there was murder, literally. Three months in a filthy convict ship, and a lot of people died. And when they got there they had to walk miles to farms where they had to work for the owners. And it was pretty bad back in Tolpuddle, too. The local magistrates – who were the landowners, of course – refused to give any support to the families of the men who had been sent to Australia, and they were nearly starving – but the Union movement had just started across the country, and people heard about what was happening in Tolpuddle, and raised lots of money to give to the families. Just goes to show that being mean is NOT a good idea.'

'So that was good,' Jake said.

'It was better than good,' Grandprof said. 'It made the Tolpuddle men famous, and there was a big petition with nearly a million signatures to get the six of them back from Australia.. So after three years they were given a free pardon, and they came back to England – but they didn't come back to Tolpuddle.'

'Why not?' Perdita said. 'What about their families?'

'They got their families to join them in Essex,' Grandprof said. 'One of them – James Loveless – a different James Loveless – wrote a pamphlet called *Church Shown Up* which told how badly the church had treated the workers. So they weren't too popular in Tolpuddle. Anyway, after a bit five of them emigrated to Canada. Poor old James had a four year old daughter, Sina, who died on the way.

'But they all did rather well. One of them, John Stanfield became a Justice of the Peace – a judge – and was a mayor and ran a hotel and a choir.'

'So they weren't really martyred after all,' Sebastian said.

'Well, no. Not really. But one of them *did* come back to Tolpuddle, a man called James Hammett – and he was a bit of an odd one out: he was not really one of the group. He wasn't a Methodist, and he had been in trouble with the police, and then he got into trouble with the police in Australia. But the odd thing is that he might not even have taken the secret oath in the first place – he let himself be arrested instead of his brother John, who *had* taken the oath.'

'Very nice of him,' said Perdita.

'Yes indeed,' said Grandprof. 'So he came back here as a builder's labourer, and he married three times, and all his three wives died – and he had seven children – one died. Then in 1875 the Agricultural Labourer's Union gave him a gold watch and a purse of gold sovereigns to celebrate his part in things, so that was good, but when he got older, his eyesight became bad, so he couldn't work. So you know what he did? He went into the Workhouse in Dorchester, which was where the very poor went, and it was a terrible place, but he did it so his family wouldn't have to look after him. And then he died, and was buried in an unmarked grave in Tolpuddle Churchyard. But, do you know, the landowners were still frightened of the Unions, so when he was buried, nobody was allowed to give a speech.' Grandprof sighed. 'You couldn't blame him if he haunted the place.

'Still, a long time after, the Unions put up a headstone for him. Maybe we can go to see it on Christmas Day.'

'Very jolly Christmassy thing to do,' Mummy said from the doorway. 'OK, everybody, bedtime.'

Jake and Josie and Dulcie kissed Grandprof, and Sebastian and Perdita stayed for a moment to pick up their books.

'Do we know what they looked like?' Perdita said. 'So I can imagine them.'

'No,' Grandprof said. 'Except for one: he was the one who came back to Tolpuddle, James Hammett. He had fair hair, a pockmarked cheek and a scar under his right eye.'

When Mummy had put their lights out, Sebastian rolled over in bed and said, in a rather low voice (for him): 'You heard what Jake said about the man in the woods.'

'The pock mark and the scar,' Perdita said.

'James Hammett,' Sebastian said. 'And Grandprof said that he wouldn't be surprised if he haunted the place,.'

'That's just a figure of speech,' Perdita said. 'We don't believe in ghosts.'

'The question is,' Sebastian said darkly, 'whether ghosts believe in us.'

24 DECEMBER
CHRISTMAS EVE

Chapter 7

In Which there is Some Log Splitting and a Ladle

Perdita padded into the kitchen to find Laura helping Granny to spread some jam on a piece of toast, Josie finishing her cornflakes, Dulcie dipping a bread soldier into her egg, and Sebastian doing research.

'Good morning, darling,' Granny said.

'Where is everybody?' Perdita said.

'If they're not in bed, they're out spodding,' Granny said. 'I saw Sebastian and Uncle Mike and Jake going out with a great big rod and some sweetcorn and Weetabix.' She shook her head slightly, just as Grannies were supposed to do. Perdita felt quite proud of her.

'Did you know, Granny,' Sebastian said, 'that the River Piddle is also called the Trent or the North River?'

'I think I prefer those names,' Granny said. 'What would you like for breakfast?' She looked around the kitchen. 'What are we going to do with all this food?'

'Eat it,' Sebastian said. 'It's got to be enough for 272 meals.'

Granny looked thoughtful, but she was used to Sebastian, so she made Perdita had a dippy egg and some hot chocolate without saying anything else.

After breakfast, Perdita went back to her room and got dressed, and there was a shout outside her window.

She looked out, and Jake was standing on the lawn – he had left a track of dark footprints on the frosty grass. He waved and pointed to something, and Perdita unclipped the catch at the bottom of the window, and pulled at the sash. To her surprise, the window slid up quite easily. She put her head down to the gap, and the cold air came in.

'Come and split logs!' Jake said. 'In the shed!' and dashed away, leaving Perdita thinking that 'dash' was another of those words that really said what it meant.

She glanced into the playroom as she came past: Josie and Dulcie and Laura were immersed – another good word – in their game of dolls. Amazing how things seemed to be going on in different worlds at the same time. It made her feel somehow out of control: that the world was looking after itself, and she didn't need to know exactly what was going on, as she did at home. It was scary and comforting at the same time.

She found Grandprof in the porch putting his boots on. 'Coming splitting?' he said, and Granny came into the hall with two empty carrier bags. 'While you're out there, could you pick up lots of little sticks for kindling. I'll put them in the AGA overnight, so they'll be dry. And don't let Grandprof fall into the stream.' She went back into the kitchen.

Perdita and Grandprof went round to the cart shed, where Uncle Mike, clearly very happy, had started the log splitter. It sounded rather like the motor mower that lived down the lane at home. Sebastian and Jake had clearly been placed at a safe distance and were sitting on an old chest-freezer. Uncle Mike picked up a huge log, and placed it on the flat bed of the splitter, and pushed two buttons – one with each thumb, simultaneously. He looked at Jake: 'That's so I can't have my hands anywhere near the splitter,' he said. As he held the buttons down, a rod with a spear-like end crept out of the orange housing of the splitter towards the end of the log. When it got there, there was slight pause, and then it dug itself into the end of the log, and there was a crack, and the log split itself into four pieces and thumped onto the floor of the shed. Uncle Mike took his thumbs off the buttons and the spear drew itself back into the housing.

'Gosh, can I do that?' said Jake, getting down off the freezer.

'No,' Uncle Mike said. 'Sit!' Jake, rather reluctantly, Perdita thought, got back onto the freezer and sat.

'That was fun,' Aunty Rill's voice said. 'Do it again!'

Perdita looked around. Aunty Rill and Uncle Zac (with Amelia in her shawl) were watching from the doorway. And, Perdita had to admit to herself, it *was* fun. Uncle Mike split several logs, and then relented, letting Jake press one button at the same time as Sebastian was pushing the other one. 'That's probably enough,' he said as the log split and fell onto the pile on the floor, and the spear hid itself away, and the motor stopped.

There was a barrow leaning against the wall, and Uncle Mike and Uncle Zac started to pile the logs into it.

Jake was exploring. 'What's this?' He was standing by a long flat table with a slit down the middle of it, and poking straight up out of the slit in the table was a very sharp-looking circular blade, with unpleasant looking teeth.

'That's serious stuff,' Uncle Mike said, coming over to admire it. 'Keep your fingers away from it!'

'But what does it do?' said Jake, only just keeping his fingers away from it.

'Well,' said Uncle Mike. 'There's a motor under there, so you have to imagine this blade spinning around very fast. It would just be a blur. Then you take a great big tree trunk, and put it on the saw bench, and then you pull this lever, and the saw blade moves down the slit in the bench towards the log, nearer and nearer – and then slices it in half. Or you can make planks by slicing slices off a big trunk.'

Behind him, Aunty Rill began to sing quietly. 'And the great big saw came nearer and nearer…'

Zac laughed. 'This afternoon's story?' he said.

'Anyway, 'Uncle Mike said, 'it's very dangerous.' He looked at it again. 'Pity it's not working, though!'

They loaded the barrow and pushed it along the terrace and round the side of the house, to where there was the pile of logs, and the two tree trunks, and the iron door in the wall. Uncle Mike bent down, slid back the bolt, and pulled at the handle.

'Of course,' he said. 'It's bolted on the inside. You couldn't have it so that people could go in and out whenever they liked.' He stood up. 'Jake – you and Sebastian run round to the front door, take your boots off, go into the dining room, and pull back the bolt on the inside of this door.'

'It says here,' Grandprof said, as Sebastian and Jake ran off – he had a booklet in his gloved hand, 'the Yule Log often was complete tree, and sometimes they would carry it into the house and stick one end into the fire. This is a much better idea.'

'Exactly,' said Uncle Mike. 'Although I don't know what they did overnight. Someone would have had to stay up and push the tree into the fireplace as it burned. Can't imagine trying to carry a burning tree back out of the front door.'

Perdita thought that she could, with ash and sparks and smoke flying.

'If we're going to do this properly,' Grandprof said, 'we ought to light it from the remains of last year's log. Apparently you kept the ashes under the bed until next year for good luck.'

'You never know,' Uncle Zac said. 'We'll organise an under-the-bed search when we get back in.'

There was a scraping noise from the iron door, and it was pushed open from the inside and Jake looked out.

'Excellent,' Uncle Mike said. 'We'll push some logs through now, and then line up these big tree bits. They can be the Yule logs. Then tomorrow, after Church, we'll light the fire and see if it works!'

'It's a very big chimney,' Jake said, pulling the logs through the iron door. 'You can see right up it.'

'In the old days,' Sebastian said, helpfully, 'they were so big that they used to send chimney boys up them to sweep them. And sometimes they'd get lost in the flues.'

'Those were the days,' Uncle Mike said, and went to get another barrow-load of logs.

~

Half an hour later, and in the wood, Perdita had collected sticks that were the right length to put in her carrier bags and the right length to fit into the AGA. There were a lot to be had, and although they were very wet and dark, they broke easily. But it wasn't easy to reach them: the undergrowth of dead – or at least, resting – brambles was too thick. She paused and straightened up. It was impossible to imagine that there was ever a road here.

She looked around for Jake, who had given up stick-finding in favour of moving logs across the stream to build a dam. Her bags were nearly full, and she went a little further down the stream to where there was a fallen tree, and its thin branches had twiggy ends that were resting just above the ground and looked as though they might easily be snapped off. She was just bending forward, when she heard something rustle in the undergrowth behind her. She looked around. The trees were very close together, and there was mist hanging between them. She looked carefully, hoping that she might see a fox, or perhaps a badger – or did they have little deer here, like they did at home sometimes? It would be a good wood to hide any of those. But nothing moved – except she heard that swishing noise again, and then she thought she saw something move, right at the edge of her sight, and it looked like a person.

And Jake called from behind her.

'Perdy – I'm going back in now.'

Perdita looked again, but there was nothing in the wood, so she pushed her way back to where Jake was standing. She had rather expected him to have stayed there all morning, or until he had finished the dam, because she knew him well enough to know that he had to finish things before he could be really happy. But he was standing soaked to halfway up his anorak and both his boots had water sloshing out of the tops.

'It's deeper than I thought,' he said, 'and I'm freezing to death.'

And so they went back to the house, but not before they had walked back along the side of the ponds so that they could see if there were any fish rising or turning in the water, but there weren't.

~

Jake was sent off for a bath, and Perdita, still not *quite* sure that the world would work if she didn't know what everyone in it was doing, pretended that she was an invisible ghost and checked all the nesting boxes. Daddy and Uncle Mike and Uncle Zac and Aunty Rill seemed to be playing an endless round of games of table-tennis in the games room, and the kitchen was agreeably full of Mummies and small people, food preparation going on at the upper level, and various complex games involving bits of trains and dolls' prams at the lower level.

Perdita had the best of times: she helped Mummy and Dulcie make the apricot stuffing, by chopping up the apricots and whizzing the breadcrumbs; then she helped Laura with her Thomas the Tank Engine Puzzle under the table, and played pushing Max up and down the corridor in the doll's pram that they had found in the playroom, and then she helped Aunty Rill make the soup for lunch. Aunty Rill shared her view of soups, and so Perdita found out how to toast spices and make croutons.

But the best bit was the gong.

When lunch was ready there were several people missing, so Mummy and Perdita went to find them. After a bit of shouting around the house, Mummy went into the utility room – the old butler's pantry – and came back with a huge metal tray, which was almost as big as Perdita, and a soup ladle almost as big as her head. And they went out onto the terrace and bashed the ladle against the tray, and it made a very satisfactory noise, and a flock of crows rose cawing from the wood, and the figures who were standing on the distant jetty waved their arms and their fishing rods. Then there was no sign of Josie and Dulcie, so Perdita stood at the bottom of the grand staircase and bashed the tray, until there were squeaks of 'Coming!' from upstairs.

Perdita went back to the kitchen feeling very pleased with herself, and squeezed into a place at the table, and Aunty Rill and Granny ladled two kind of soup – Granny's and Aunty Rill's, and into the kitchen came Dulcie and Josie, each carrying a large china chamber pot.

There was a moment of complete silence, and then Josie said: 'Grandprof told us that we should look under all the beds to see if there was last year's Yule log. But there wasn't. But we found these. What are they for?'

'Grandprof will explain after lunch,' Granny said firmly, and after lunch, Grandprof stopped in the corridor and explained to Dulcie and Josie (and Perdita, who was watching) that in the Old Days – and they were even older days than his old days – people had kept chamber pots under their beds because they didn't have inside loos, and how the servants had the job of carrying the full ones downstairs in the morning. Both Dulcie and Josie decided that they were going to keep them under their beds to use in the night, and Grandprof said that he hadn't heard that.

At this point Perdita thought that it was only kind to take Grandprof's hand and lead him into the library, where Daddy was settling everyone down for the latest episode of *A Christmas Carol*. They had got as far as when Scrooge wakes up for the second time and finds out what Christmas can be like when people set out to enjoy it.

'It was his own room. There was no doubt about that.
But it had undergone a surprising transformation.
The walls and ceiling were so hung with living green,
that it looked a perfect grove; from every part of
which, bright gleaming berries glistened. The crisp
leaves of holly, mistletoe, and Josie reflected back the
light, as if so many little mirrors had been scattered
there; and such a mighty blaze went roaring up the
chimney, as that dull petrification of a hearth had
never known in Scrooge's time, or Marley's, or for
many and many a winter season gone. Heaped up
on the floor, to form a kind of throne, were turkeys,
geese, game, poultry, brawn, great joints of meat,
sucking-pigs, long wreaths of sausages, mince pies,
plum-puddings, barrels of oysters, red-hot chestnuts,
cherry-cheeked apples, juicy oranges, luscious pears,
immense twelfth-cakes, and seething bowls of punch,
that made the chamber dim with their delicious
steam. In easy state upon this couch, there sat a jolly
Giant, glorious to see; who bore a glowing torch, in
shape not unlike Plenty's horn, and held it up, high

up, to shed its light on Scrooge, as he came peeping round the door.

"Come in!" exclaimed the Ghost. 'Come in! and know me better, man!'

Scrooge entered timidly, and hung his head before this Spirit. He was not the dogged Scrooge he had been; and though the Spirit's eyes were clear and kind, he did not like to meet them.

"I am the Ghost of Christmas Present," said the Spirit. "Look upon me!"

Scrooge reverently did so. It was clothed in one simple green robe, or mantle, bordered with white fur. This garment hung so loosely on the figure, that its capacious breast was bare, as if disdaining to be warded or concealed by any artifice. Its feet, observable beneath the ample folds of the garment, were also bare; and on its head it wore no other covering than a holly wreath, set here and there with shining icicles. Its dark brown curls were long and free; free as its genial face, its sparkling eye, its open hand, its cheery voice, its unconstrained demeanour, and its joyful air. Girded round its middle was an antique scabbard; but no sword was in it, and the ancient sheath was eaten up with rust.'

'There you go,' Daddy said. 'And tomorrow we'll find out what happened to the old misery.'

Chapter 8

In Which Perdita Loses Jake and Sees Some Clouds

What happened next was really Perdita's fault, everyone decided afterwards, because when everyone else went off in various directions to do various things, she stayed in front of the fire and re-read *A Christmas Carol* up to the page they had stopped at. Then she found that there was a pile of Christmas picture books beside the sofa, so she read *Alfie's Christmas*, and *Lucy and Tom's Christmas*, and several others, and then she went to the shelves and looked at the backs of lots of books. She had just started to read *The Water Babies*, when Jake came in and sat down beside her on the floor.

He didn't look happy.

Perdita said, 'What's wrong?' and Jake explained at some length that after this morning, when he and Uncle Mike and Sebastian had stood on the jetty not catching anything, they had decided to do some fishing from the dinghy. So they had got the oars from the shed, and turned the boat the right way up, and they had got the short fishing rods, and some more sweetcorn from Granny, for bait. Then they had very quietly rowed out onto the pond, and they had sat for an hour, getting colder and colder. And they fished where they had ground-baited, and they fished where they had not ground-baited, and they got colder and colder and colder and absolutely nothing happened.

So they had pulled the boat out of the water and had come back into the house. Uncle Mike had gone to have a shower, and Sebastian had gone to help in the kitchen, and he, Jake, had gone down to the games room to play skittles. But now Aunty Rill and Uncle Zac and Perdita's Mummy and Daddy were playing an endless game of table-tennis that seemed to involve running around the table between pings and pongs. He had tried to play skittles, but it wasn't much fun on his own, especially when he had to walk down and set the skittles up himself every time he knocked them down. And he couldn't work out how to make the pool table give up any balls, and in the end he thought he might explore the cellars, but the moment he put his hand on the door handle, Aunty Rill said, 'You'd better not go in there, Jake. Out of bounds,' and went on playing.

So, Jake said, looking gloomily into the fire, here he was.

He looked over at Perdita. 'Whatcha reading?'

'*The Water Babies*,' Perdita said. 'It's about a boy who's a chimney sweep in the days when they made boys go up the chimneys. It's awful.

'How many chimneys Tom swept I cannot say; but he swept so many that he got quite tired, and puzzled too, for they were not like the town flues to which he was accustomed, but such as you would find – if you would only get up them and look, which perhaps you would not like to do – in old country-houses, large and crooked chimneys, which had been altered

again and again, till they ran one into another, …
So Tom fairly lost his way in them; not that he cared much for that, though he was in pitchy darkness, for he was as much at home in a chimney as a mole is underground; but at last, coming down as he thought the right chimney, he came down the wrong one, and found himself standing on the hearthrug in a room the like of which he had never seen before.'

'Terrible,' Jake said. They sat there for a little while, and then Perdita went on to read about how Tom the sweep found himself in the little girl's white room, and when she next looked up, Jake had gone.

She felt rather sad for him, though, and put her book down and went out into the hall. There was no Jake, but Dulcie and Josie and Sebastian were playing mountain climbing on the stairs. They had taken all their dressing gown cords and tied them together into a mountain rope, and had their backpacks on, and were moving from stair to stair very slowly.

'Have you seen Jake?' Perdita asked.

'He went into the dining room,' Sebastian said. He thought for a moment. 'Don't know what he's doing in there.'

With a funny feeling that she might know, Perdita crossed the hall and went into the room. There was no sign of Jake. The long table and all its chairs were undisturbed. She looked under the big dresser. No sign. She looked behind the curtains, in case he was hiding on one of the window sills, but nobody there.

And then she saw that one of the fire-irons was lying in the hearth, instead of in its holder, and the electric fire was no longer in the centre of the hearth. She stepped into the hearth and looked up the chimney. It went upwards and narrowed and she could see a square of grey sky against the blackness.

Sebastian, who had come in behind her, with Dulcie and Josie in tow, said, 'Do you think he could have?' He took his torch out of his backpack and pointed it straight up the chimney. Then he shook his head. 'He couldn't have gone up there,' he said. 'There's no marks on the soot. And no footholds.'

'Is there a shelf or something?' Perdita said. She knew that all old chimneys had a shelf just about where you could reach it and there was usually something on it, but Sebastian was on another track.

'That's where he went,' and pointed to metal square door for the Yule log. If you looked carefully, you could see that it wasn't quite shut.

'Uncle Mike mustn't have slid the outside bolt,' Perdita said.

'Why should he?' Sebastian said. 'It's the inside one that matters.' Even in that moment, Perdita remembered that on her bedroom door at home there was a small bolt on the *outside*. It had been there when they moved in, and nobody could work out what it was for.

'Come on,' said Sebastian. 'Let's see where he's gone,' and he pulled the iron door open and he and Perdita – and Josie and Dulcie, who were still attached to Sebastian by the mountain rope – bent and wriggled through it, getting soot on their backpacks.

Outside, it was already falling dark, but they could see across the lawns to the woods. Nothing moved. Sebastian started to say that he must have gone round to the front door when they heard a small voice from a long way above them. They looked up, and above them the chimney rose up, getting narrower, and every time it narrowed, there were two small steps in the stonework. Perdita thought that if you were Jake, it must have looked very tempting to climb. Perhaps four metres up, the chimney met the steep slope of the roof, and that went up and up until it met the battlements. And leaning over, and waving his arm, was Jake. His voice floated to them.

'I can't get down.'

Perdita and Sebastian looked at eachother and thought the same thought. If Jake was actually admitting that he couldn't get down, then he really was stuck. They also had the same thought about calling for grown-up help.

Perdita said, firmly, to Dulcie and Josie. 'Jake is on the roof, so we'd better go up to the attic and let him in. Race you!' Sebastian thoughtfully and remarkably quickly untied his dressing gown cord from Dulcie and they all wriggled back through the iron door. On the stairs, they passed Grandprof coming down, but he simply helpfully stood to one side to let them go by, and then went on down the stairs without saying anything. Dulcie and Josie had a head start, but they arrived at the attic door together.

Sebastian pushed open the door and felt for the light switch, and then changed his mind, and they stood still until their eyes could see the shape of the window at the far end of the attic, and the lines of light outlining the dormer windows that looked out onto the roof.

There was a scraping on the slates, and then a tapping. Sebastian switched on his torch, and they followed the sound, being careful to keep their feet on the planking. Halfway along the attic, there was a dormer window that had not been boarded up, but its glass was grey on the inside with spiders' webs and dust, and green on the outside with moss and lichen. They could just see Jake crouched against it. He stopped tapping.

Sebastian pointed his torch. The window was in two parts and once upon a time would have opened inwards. Where the two halves met, there was a metal catch which had been painted over. Perdita twisted it, but it was completely stuck. She took Sebastian's torch and went back to the attic door and switched on the light. On the bench by the end of the railway layout, there was a cardboard box of tools, and in it was a large hammer, with a curved head. She took it back to the window.

'You're not going to break the glass are you?' said Dulcie, in a very cheerful voice, but Perdita could only think of a very serious mess and some very dangerous glass shards if she did, so she hooked the curved end of the hammer under the catch, and levered it back. The screws holding it pulled softly out of the rotten wood, Jake leaned on the windows, and they bent inwards, rather than opening, because the hinges had been painted over too, and then the screws of the left hand window pulled out of the window frames. Sebastian caught the window as it started to fall, lowered it to the ground, and leant it against the wall.

Jake seemed happy enough to see them, but not particularly grateful, and showed no sign of being rescued and climbing into the attic. Rather the reverse.

'Come and see,' he said, and before Perdita could stop them, Sebastian and Dulcie and Josie had scrambled – another good word – out onto the roof. She decided that even if she didn't like heights, she was a Big Sister and Big Sisters did not let their Little Sisters fall of roofs, and that if any Little Sister was likely to fall of a roof then that little sister might well be Dulcie, so she climbed out after them.

They were on a small flat area between all the gables and the chimneys, with the low wall of battlements. And when you got to the edges, there was a sharp drop to the sloping roof, and then another longer drop to the ground. It seemed a very very long way down, and for a moment Perdita couldn't take a breath, but she grabbed hold of Dulcie's backpack and said, 'Just one look and then we're going back inside.'

'Can't get back down,' Jake said cheerfully. 'Too slippy. But look!'

They looked, in the cold winter light of a low, grey, misted early moon, out over the top of the woods and then across the flat valley with the thread of the river between the flat fields and then across to Tolpuddle and the church. But beyond that, and above it all there was the darkest sky any of them had ever seen.

'Is it a storm?' Josie said. She seemed quite untroubled by the height, and Perdita was almost jealous.

'It's snow coming,' Sebastian said firmly. 'Altostratus.'

'Let's get back inside,' Perdita said, faintly, and they climbed back into the attic.

Jake looked at the window and out at the roof. 'Whatever you do,' he said, 'don't tell my Mummy.'

~

They walked into the warm, teatime-smelling kitchen. Uncle Mike and Daddy were making sandwiches. Daddy was buttering, and Uncle Mike was holding a jar of Granny's strawberry jam and a spoon. The whole of the long table was covered in clean tea towels that were obviously covering differently-shaped and interesting things. Nobody else seemed to be there.

'Hi, Dulcie,' Daddy said. 'What you been doing all day?'

'We've been on the roof,' Dulcie said brightly. 'Right on the top. Tip top. You can see for miles.'

Daddy stopped with the butter knife in the air. 'And how did you get out there?'

Perdita looked around at Jake, who was starting to back slowly out of the kitchen.

'Jake climbed all the way up the outside of the chimney,' Dulcie said, full of admiration. 'And Perdita had to knock a window out so he could come in. What's for tea?'

'Sandwiches,' Daddy said.

'We didn't break anything,' Perdita said to Uncle Mike, 'but I'm afraid we couldn't get the window back in.'

'Hmn,' Uncle Mike said. 'You'd better show me, so I can mend it. No, just Perdita.' He put the jar of jam down and looked around. Jake had disappeared.

Daddy looked at the butter knife, and then went on buttering.

'Do you know, Daddy,' Sebastian said. 'I think it's going to snow.'

~

Perdita came down the stairs with Uncle Mike feeling slightly pleased with herself, because he had said so many nice things about how sensible she had been. She tried not to feel *too* pleased because how sensible she had been also implied how not sensible someone else had been, and she knew that if you thought like that then there might be arguments that lasted for chapter after chapter.

As they came into the hall they met Dulcie and Laura and Aunty Fee, who was carrying Amelia.

'Teatime! Teatime!' said Dulcie and Laura said 'Teatime!' and they trotted off towards the kitchen.

Perdita said, 'I'll be there in a minute,' and darted – which was another good word – into the dining room. There was a distinct cold draught coming from the iron door in the back of the fireplace. She stepped in, and started to bend down to close it, when a thought struck her and she straighten up, and reached as high as she could to the stone shelf inside the chimney, and walked her fingers along it. (She thought afterwards that it was a good job she had been in a hurry, because if she had had time to think about it, she might have worried that there was something sitting on the shelf waiting to nibble her fingers.) And, to her amazement, there *was* something there – something soft and knobbly. She very carefully tugged at it, and a small purse fell off the shelf and landed with a small ping in the fireplace. Perdita picked it up and wondered what to do with it. The best thing would be to show it to everybody straight away, but to judge from the people buzzing around the kitchen, this might not be the moment. So she stepped out of the hearth and put the sooty purse carefully on the top of one of the low cupboards that ran around the room.

Then she stepped back into the hearth and started to close the iron door. But before she slid the bolt across, something made her open it slightly, so that, crouching, she could look out at the darkening lawns.

She felt herself smiling, and thinking of a quotation from one of her favourite books: 'Softly at first, as if it hardly meant it, the snow began to fall.'

And then she went into the kitchen for tea.

Chapter 9

In which there is a Great Big Saw and more About Uncle Charlie

Perdita said, thinking about it afterwards, that this was her second favourite meal of the whole holidays. You had to stand on a chair to see it all properly, so they all stood on chairs while the grown-ups were making rather less-interesting things like cups of tea. Down the middle of the long kitchen table were large white plates, with piles of little vegetarian sausage rolls, and prunes wrapped in crispy bacon, which were called devils on horseback, Marmite fingers, hard-boiled eggs, little sausages glistening (this was, Perdita thought, a great day for Really Good Words) with honey, and little jam sandwiches, and bowls of crisps of different colours. And fizzy lemonade, which they never had at home.

Jake wanted to take his plate and eat everything on the floor of the playroom with the lights out, but Granny said that the rule was that everyone had to be altogether and if you weren't together you couldn't have any food, so he gave in.

And it was lovely, although even as she was eating, there was something worrying at the back of her mind. Just a niggle, as if somewhere outside the warm and happy kitchen there was something she should be worried about. But there was so much fun going on that she filed the feeling away. Maybe she could think about it in bed tonight.

After what seemed about five minutes, in which all the things on the table miraculously disappeared, and they had all taken their plates to the dishwasher until that was full, and then piled them on the draining board by the sink, where Daddy was washing up and Uncle Zac was drying up, it was time for The Rehearsal.

It had been Granny's idea that they should do another play for Christmas, when they were all together. They hadn't all been together for Christmas since they had been very little, and then they'd made a nativity play, and Jake and Perdita had dressed in their dressing-gowns, and had been shepherds, and Josie had been a sheep, and Sebastian had been a star, until he fell off the back of the sofa, and Dulcie had been the baby Jesus. But Granny thought that they could do a lot better now they were more grown up.

And so Grandprof had been asked, or told, to write a play for them. They'd done little plays quite a lot when they got together in the summer, and pulled a sheet across Jake's bedroom. Those plays tended to be about pirates and involved a lot of jumping off beds and running around with swords, and not many words to learn, and most of the time nobody knew what was going to happen next – neither the actors nor the audience, and it was very fun.

But this time Grandprof had written a proper script and had sent it round to all the families a couple of weeks ago (the grown-ups were not allowed to see it) so that Jake and Josie and Perdita and Sebastian and Dulcie could learn their parts. And so now they went upstairs with Grandprof to Mummy and Daddy's room, which was the biggest, and went through the play. Even Laura, as long as she could hold Josie's hand, was quite good at it, and everybody agreed that they weren't going to tell anybody about it (and Dulcie promised especially) until tomorrow, when they were going to perform it after lunch. But they did need a lamb, a baby Jesus, a star, and a crib. Dulcie said they could have her lamb as long as they didn't frighten it. Aunty Fee said that Amelia could play the baby Jesus as long as she was asleep, and Uncle Zac said that if she wasn't they could use his big torch. There was a star on top of the Christmas tree, and as Uncle Mike was so tall that he could easily reach it, they stopped worrying about that. And Josie found a wicker washing basket in the Butler's Pantry. So that all they needed to do was write the programmes, which they did on the kitchen table until it was bath time.

This was a little more orderly than the previous night, with Mummy and Granny and Aunty Cass in charge, and when they all came down to the library, Uncle Zac and Laura were waiting for them. Mummy and Daddy and Grandprof sidled in and sat behind them.

'This is *terrible* story,' Uncle Zac said, 'are you ready?'

They all nodded. Uncle Zac looked around the room and lowered his voice.

'It's about a very wicked mill owner. He owned a mill just like the one in the woods, except that it was much bigger, and it had a big mill pond and the water ran under the mill in a dark tunnel, and turned a great big mill wheel. And what do you think the mill wheel did?'

'It ground corn,' said Josie.

'Noooo,' Uncle Zac said. 'It was a saw mill, and the mill wheel turned a huge great circular saw which whizzed round and round – just like the one in the cart shed, except much much bigger and much much sharper! And you set that saw going and you put a log on the saw table, and the saw whizzed and came nearer and nearer to the log and sawed it in two – zizzz-chunk – or cut it into planks – zizzz, shwoop, schwoop.

'Now, just down the road from the mill lived a beautiful girl called Vera, and the wicked owner of the saw mill wanted her to be his wife. But she said, "Oh, no! Never! I will never be your wife! You are old and ugly and smelly: I'm going to marry my boyfriend, handsome Jack the woodman!"

'Well, you can imagine that the villainous old mill owner was not happy about that, so he plotted and plotted to find a way to make little Vera his wife.

'Now, every day, Vera and Jack would walk hand in had down by the millstream, and one day the villainous owner of the saw mill crept through the woods behind them and hit poor Jack on the head with his walking stick! Then he threw him into the millstream, and dragged poor Vera into the saw mill. Then he took off his belt and tied her down to the saw bench – and *turned on the machinery*.

And Uncle Zac began to sing … and Mummy and Grandprof joined in….

'And the great big saw came nearer and nearer
And nearer and nearer and nearer
"Be my wife or you will be cut in two"
Said the villain to poor little Vera.'

Uncle Zac said: 'And she said, "No! No! You can cut me in half if you like, but when I get to heaven the angels will stick me together again!"'

And this time, they all joined in.

'And the great big saw came nearer and nearer
And nearer and nearer and nearer
"Be my wife or you will be cut in two"
Said the villain to poor little Vera.'

'But Vera said: "I don't care if you cut me into planks, I'll never marry you!"'

'And the great big saw came nearer and nearer
And nearer and nearer and nearer
And the great big saw came nearer and nearer
And nearer and nearer and nearer.'

'But – remember handsome Jack, the woodman?' Uncle Zac said. 'He'd been swept down the stream and right underneath the mill – and just before he got to the great mill wheel, the water woke him up, and he climbed up a ladder and up through a trapdoor, and searched around to try to find Vera.'

'And the great big saw came nearer and nearer
And nearer and nearer and nearer…'

'Poor Vera was about to be cut right in half when Jack burst into the room and shouted, "Hands up, you villain! I have a gun!" And the villainous saw mill owner put his hands up! But, you remember that the villain had taken his belt off to tie Vera down with, so when he put his hands up, his trousers fell down. And when he was bending down to pull them up again, Jack gave him a good kick and he fell right out of the window and was drowned in the millpond.'

'And the great big saw came nearer and nearer
And nearer and nearer and nearer…'

By this time, Dulcie was jumping up and down and Perdita was holding on to the arm of the sofa so hard that her hands were beginning to hurt,

'So then Jack said, "But what are we going to do? I can't marry you if you've been sawn in two" and Vera shouted "STOP THE MACHINE, YOU IDIOT!"

'And the great big saw came nearer and nearer
And nearer and nearer and nearer … and
STOPPED!'

There was a collective sigh of relief. 'And they got married and lived happily ever after' Uncle Zac said, 'and they never went near the saw mill again. And the years went by, and it fell down, and you've seen what it looks like now.'

Then it was time to send their Christmas present lists to Father Christmas, so they sat in front of the fire, and Uncle Mike took the fireguard away, and they took turns to read out their lists and to put them into the fire and watch them burn, so that when the smoke came out of the top of the chimney, Father Christmas would read it and get the right presents to the right people. Laura was rather worried about this, and wouldn't let go of her list, and Max, who had been playing with Aunty Rill in the playroom, and had been brought in at the last minute, kept on trying to dance into the fire, and Jake wanted to poke every one of the messages with the poker, but at last it was done.

The next thing was that they had to leave a glass of something and some mince pies for Father Christmas and some carrots for the reindeer. Aunty Cass had got these ready in front of the dining room fireplace. 'After all,' she said, 'it's the biggest chimney, and it hasn't had a fire in it, so Father Christmas won't get stuck or singed.'

'And now,' Mummy said, 'It's time for bed. And as it's Christmas Eve, everybody has to go to bed quietly and go to sleep, otherwise Father Christmas *might not come*!'

Perdita and Sebastian and Dulcie duly went to their bathroom and cleaned their teeth, and went to bed. There was some running about on the landing and some thumping, and then they heard Uncle Mike's calm voice, and things went quiet for a bit, and then there was more thumping and Aunty Cass came up and had a discussion with Jake and Josie.

Perdita, who was not used to disorder in the evenings, found this all just a little unsettling (and Dulcie was worried in case Father Christmas would think it was them not behaving properly) so when, a little bit later, Daddy put his head round the bathroom door and said, 'Ready for lights out?' Perdita said, 'Not really,' and Sebastian said: 'We all feel a bit … *rushed*. I mean,' he said, 'it's *fun*, but it's all a bit…' he thought about it … '*busy*.'

Perdita knew what he meant. It was as if, at home, the seas were always calm, and here they were always choppy. Not that everything wasn't nice, because it was: it was just that there was a *lot* of everything. You didn't have time to breathe.

Daddy nodded and sat down at the foot of the bed. 'What this bedroom needs,' he said, 'is an Uncle Charlie story.'

Dulcie cuddled her lamb, and Sebastian put the book he was reading onto his bedside table, and Perdita drew her knees up under her duvet.

'Well,' Daddy said, 'you remember the story about Uncle Charlie and Great-Great Granny's pies and the broken loo pipe?' They all nodded, and Dulcie said, 'Yuckky.'

'But, you know,'' Daddy said, 'poor old Charlie was very unlucky when it came to loos and things, even when he was grown up.' He looked round to see if Mummy was in their bedroom, but she wasn't, so he went on.

'Not long after the pies and the pipe, Charlie joined the Boy Scouts. He wasn't very good at it, and he didn't like camping because he could never get his tent to stay up, but the worst thing was the loos. It wasn't like today, when you go to a camp site and you have nice clean flush loos. What they used to do in those days was dig a sort of ditch, and then put a pole across it, sideways, and when you wanted to go, you sat on the pole and …'

Sebastian said: 'I bet he fell in.'

'He did,' Daddy said. 'Twice. So that was the end of the Scouts for him. Great-Great Granny said she couldn't be doing with him coming home covered in… Well, you know…

'And it didn't change when he grew up. So when Great-Grandfather – that's Grandprof's daddy – got married to Great Granny, they used to come and stay on the farm at weekends, because Great-Grandfather had moved away by then. The first night they were there, they went to bed, upstairs of course, and Great Granny woke up in the middle of the night, and there was a low ghostly noise outside the window.'

'What was it?' Dulcie said. 'A ghost?'

'I thought you were asleep,' Daddy said.

'I am,' Dulcie said. 'This is lamb speaking.'

'Well,' Daddy said, 'Great Granny didn't know what it was, and she didn't like to wake Great-Grandfather, so she didn't say anything. But then the next night, there was a strange scratching at the window. This time, she got out of bed, and tiptoed up to the window, and she lifted the side of the curtain, slowly, slowly, just a bit, and...' He paused... 'And she was just in time to see Uncle Charlie sneaking away with a ladder under his arm. He'd been climbing up and making ghostly noises and scratchings to scare her. Well, she thought, so that's how it is, and she had an idea. You know, in those days, they only had the one loo – you remember – and after the disaster with the pies, they didn't get it repaired – so they used to have chamber pots.'

'Like the ones we found under the bed,' Dulcie said.

'Just like them,' Daddy said.

'Pooh, that's disgusting,' Dulcie said.

'Not just pooh,' Perdita said.

'They had lids,' Daddy said. 'Anyway, the next night, Great Granny lay awake, and around midnight, she heard this ghostly laughing outside the window, so she got out of bed and got the chamber pot out from under the bed...'

'And took the lid off,' said Sebastian.

'And took the lid off,' said Daddy, 'and she opened the window, and Uncle Charlie was halfway down the ladder. Of course he looked up, and she...'

'Was it full?' Perdita said.

'Of course.'

Mummy had come into the bathroom and had been listening.

'Just like at home,' she said,

'That's the idea,' Daddy said.

~

Something woke Perdita in the night, and it took her a moment to realise that it was the light. She lay for another moment looking at the ceiling, which seemed to have light glowing out of it. That couldn't be right, so she slipped out of bed and tiptoed to the curtain, and lifted the edge. At first she thought she couldn't see anything, and then she realised that everything was dark and light at the same time. The light from the bathroom window sent a narrow shape onto the pale lawns, and there were dark flakes drifting and flowing.

She stood for a long time looking at them, and then she went back to bed, and got her torch and picked up a green book from the floor, and pulled the covers over her head, and read by torchlight.

Dorothea woke with a dreadful fear that she had overslept. The room was full of light. The ceiling gleamed white. The blue flowers that made a pattern on the wall-paper … were somehow brighter than they had been on any other morning. Had the sun been up a long time? And then, looking out at the window, Dorothea saw the white snow deep across the hill. She leapt out of bed and ran to the window. There was a new world. Everything was white and somehow still. Everything was holding its breath.

Perdita smiled and switched the torch off, and carefully laid the book on the carpet and went to sleep, smiling.

25 DECEMBER

CHRISTMAS DAY

Chapter 10

In Which Perdita Realises What's Wrong
and Does Something About It

It was a quarter past nine on Christmas morning, and Perdita was exhausted already.

They had woken to deep snow on the lawns and the trees and the terrace, and they'd opened their stockings on Mummy and Daddy's bed. Then they had visited Jake and Josie and Max and looked at *their* stockings, and had visited Granny and Grandprof and to help them to open *their* stockings. (And they'd had their first chocolate of the day – a Malteser each – because Grandprof said what was the point of having Christmas chocolate in your Christmas stocking if you couldn't eat it on Christmas Day?) And then Perdita had looked after Laura while Aunty Fee changed Amelia. Then they all had hot chocolate in the kitchen and put their waterproofs and boots on, and floundered out into the snow.

It was still snowing, although not as hard as it had been, and they made a big snowman and perched him on the edge of the ha-ha, so that when they left in three days' time they could push him over the edge. Then they had a snowball fight, and made some snow stars by falling backwards into the snow. And then they'd been called indoors, and Jake and Dulcie had gone into Aunty Rill's room with two snowballs, and put them down her neck, and had been chased all over the house.

After that there was a mad breakfast with Aunty Rill frying ham, and Aunty Cass baking scones, and then Granny shooed them out of the kitchen, as Grannies are supposed to do, and then they all had to go and find their church clothes.

That was how Perdita found herself in the library, sitting in front of the fire, which had fresh logs on it, burning cleanly – she had a vague impression of Uncle Zac passing down the corridor with armfuls of logs – and waiting for everyone else to get ready. She felt breathless inside, which was a nice thing, but it was also nice just to be alone for a minute. She sat back on the sofa and opened one of the books that she had got in her stocking. She'd read it before, of course, having got it from the library, but this was a nice new shiny copy, and the paper was so white that it looked almost blue. She read:

'Merry Christmas, Marmee! Many of them!
Thank you for our books. We read some, and mean to
every day,' they all cried in chorus.
'Merry Christmas, little daughters! I'm glad you
began at once, and hope you will keep on. But I want
to say one word before we sit down. Not far away
from here lies a poor woman with a little newborn
baby. Six children are huddled into one bed to keep
from freezing, for they have no fire. There is nothing
to eat over there, and the oldest boy came to tell me

they were suffering hunger and cold. My girls, will you give them your breakfast as a Christmas present?'

They were all unusually hungry, having waited nearly an hour, and for a minute no one spoke, only a minute, for Jo exclaimed impetuously, 'I'm so glad you came before we began!'

'May I go and help carry the things to the poor little children?' asked Beth eagerly.

'I shall take the cream and the muffins,' added Amy, heroically giving up the article she most liked.

Meg was already covering the buckwheats, and piling the bread into one big plate.

'I thought you'd do it,' said Mrs. March, smiling as if satisfied. 'You shall all go and help me, and when we come back we will have bread and milk for breakfast, and make it up at dinnertime.'

They were soon ready, and the procession set out. Fortunately it was early, and they went through back streets, so few people saw them, and no one laughed at the queer party.

A poor, bare, miserable room it was, with broken windows, no fire, ragged bedclothes, a sick mother, wailing baby, and a group of pale, hungry children cuddled under one old quilt, trying to keep warm.

How the big eyes stared and the blue lips smiled as the girls went in.

'Ach, mein Gott! It is good angels come to us!' said the poor woman, crying for joy.

'Funny angels in hoods and mittens,' said Jo, and set them to laughing.

In a few minutes it really did seem as if kind spirits had been at work there. Hannah, who had carried wood, made a fire, and stopped up the broken panes with old hats and her own cloak. Mrs. March gave the mother tea and gruel, and comforted her with promises of help, while she dressed the little baby as tenderly as if it had been her own. The girls meantime spread the table, set the children round the fire, and fed them like so many hungry birds, laughing, talking, and trying to understand the funny broken English.

'Das ist gut!' 'Die Engel-kinder!' cried the poor things as they ate and warmed their purple hands at the comfortable blaze. The girls had never been called angel children before, and thought it very agreeable … That was a very happy breakfast, though they didn't get any of it. And when they went away, leaving comfort behind, I think there were not in all the city four merrier people than the hungry little girls who gave away their breakfasts and contented themselves with bread and milk on Christmas morning.

'That's loving our neighbour better than ourselves, and I like it,' said Meg.

Perdita was pondering on this when Aunty Fee came in with Amelia. 'You're looking a little sad,' she said. Perdita held the book up.

Aunty Fee sat down and began to feed the baby. 'I know,' she said. 'It's difficult isn't it. We're so happy and lucky. I remember when your Mummy and me and Aunty Cass and Aunty Rill were little, we used to worry about that too.'

'Did you ever go and give your breakfast to poor people?'

'I don't think so,' Aunty Fee said. 'I don't think we knew any poor people. You'd better ask Granny. I know we used to drive miles and miles to see Great Granny so she wouldn't be lonely at Christmas, but I suppose that was as much for our benefit, because we liked seeing her.'

Perdita looked at the fire.

'But what you could do,' Aunty Fee said, 'is after church, why don't you ask the Vicar if she knows anyone who might like a visit. Especially now it's all snowy. There might be old people in the village who can't get out. She'd know.'

Which was all very well, Perdita thought, as she left her book and the warm fire and Aunty Fee, and went to put her boots on. But you can't just *say* that. It was not that Vicars bothered her – there were enough in the family, after all. But it sounded – what was Daddy's least favourite word – *patronising*.

It was still snowing, although a little more lazily, when, as Granny put it, they were all booted and spurred – all except Aunty Fee, who was allowed to sleep in front of the library fire with the baby in the crib – and they set out across the snowy gravel drive, where it was quite difficult to walk. But Jake and Uncle Mike and Daddy went ahead to clear a path, and the rest of them followed them, singing 'In his master's steps they trod where the snow lay dinted.'

The lane was no better than the drive, and nothing had driven along it that morning. When they got to the junction where the road divided, there were a few tracks on the road across the valley, but that only made it more slippery where the tyres had packed the snow down.

On either side of the road there was not a speck of green, not even tall clumps of dead grass. The snow lay – well, Perdita thought – like snow, but glowing cold, as if the light were coming from under the snow rather than out of the sky. They had to be careful to keep to the middle of the road, because you couldn't see where the ditches were. But, as Uncle Zac said, it was like taking several puppies for a walk: Josie and Sebastian and Jake kept running and sliding ahead, and Dulcie tried to keep up with them and then Laura had to try running after Dulcie. Halfway across the valley, where the little river, now looking rather black, ran slowly between the piles of snow, two cars came by, and they had to all gather together on one side of the road in a gateway as they slithered past. There was nothing slushy about this snow.

~

They walked up the path through the churchyard, with Grandprof and Sebastian trying to outbore eachother in the most friendly way.

'Look, it's cobflint and rubble with ashlar dressings, like the church in …'

'Apparently, it's got a blocked up door which was called the sin door and that's where the evil spirits were let out during christenings.'

'St John the Evangelist wrote the Gospel of St John, and he was the disciple who Jesus loved.'

'Didn't he love them all?' Daddy said, and they came to the porch, where the Vicar was greeting people. She had a genuine sort of smile.

'Well done! I wasn't sure anybody would make it with all this snow,' she said,

Granny said, 'Did you have a good Midnight Mass?'

'Even that wasn't as good as usual,' the Vicar said. 'The snow was beginning to build up, so that kept a lot of people away.'

But the Church was quite warm – at least it had that churchy kind of warmth that, Perdita thought, was warm around your feet but seemed to give up halfway along your back.

There was a carved stone tomb against the wall where they were sitting. Sebastian read out the inscription.

'SI QUIS AMAT XPM
QUI SARCOPHAGUM VIDET ISTUM
DICAT PRESBITERO
REQUIEN DA CHRISTE PHILIPPO'

Mummy said, 'If any lover of Christ should see this tombstone, let him say "Grant rest, O Christ, to Philip the priest"'.

'I wonder who he was,' Perdita said, thinking that it was rather an odd thing to say, because you would have thought that anyone who was in a church, looking at gravestones, would have been a lover of Christ anyway.

'Twelfth century priest,' Grandprof said.

'I'm not bringing you again,' Mummy said.

As they made up about a third of the congregation, something that Perdita was quite used to when her family went to church together, she sang especially loudly to make up for all the empty pews and to cheer the Vicar up.

The sermon was short and Christmassy, and was about looking after people who couldn't get out in the bad weather, which made it rather easier for Perdita to wait until almost everybody had gone at the end of the service, so she could say to the Vicar, 'Excuse me. But do you know of anybody who would like a visit? We're staying at Tolpuddle Grange and I was, we were, wondering if anybody was lonely, or poor.' It sounded ridiculous, but she kept her voice as loud as she could, even if it seemed to want to get smaller.

The Vicar looked at her. 'Like in *Little Women*?' she said.

'Well, we do seem to have such a lot of everything,' Perdita said.

'Well, bless your heart o' gold!' the Vicar said. 'You'll make a fine considering wench some market day. Sorry. Bad habit, quoting.'

'I know that,' Perdita said. 'That's Puck.'

The Vicar looked at her with rather more attention. And respect. 'It is. It is,' she said. 'You're staying at the Grange?'

Perdita felt, rather than saw, Aunty Rill drifting up behind her into a supportive position, and nodded, yes.

'Well, we're very well catered for when it comes to looking after the poor and lonely,' the Vicar said. 'But…' she paused and smiled, almost mischievously – another thing, Perdita thought, that people don't do much outside books. 'There are two old ladies – perhaps I shouldn't call them that – at High Puddle Farm just along the lane from you. They very rarely miss anything at Church, but they haven't appeared today – or last night – so I was about to give them a ring. And people don't visit *them* as much as they deserve. Perhaps you could walk up and see if they're OK. I'll ring them and you might visit on Boxing Day or the day after if they'd like you to. I'll let you know.' She shook hands with her, and with Aunty Rill, who was looking very pleased about something, and they went out into the churchyard.

They had to follow the tracks in the snow to find Grandprof, who had taken the family round to see the grave of James Hammett, the Martyr who had come back to Tolpuddle, but it seemed that seeing the grave took only about five seconds, and everyone was heading for the gate by the time they got there. But Perdita, who liked graveyards, stood and read the inscription carefully.

JAMES HAMMETT, TOLPUDDLE MARTYR,
PIONEER OF TRADES UNIONISM,
CHAMPION OF FREEDOM. BORN 11
DECEMBER 1811. DIED 21 NOVEMBER 1891

Then she took Aunty Rill's gloved hand, and they followed the others.

On the way back, Perdita found herself walking with Jake behind Uncle Mike and Daddy and Uncle Zac, which was a good place to walk, because although there wasn't heat in the very sod, at least the snow was dinted, and you could walk where Uncle Mike's huge wellies had stamped the snow down.

There was a discussion going on about the Yule log and the fire in the dining room, and the idea that you would open the metal door at the back of the fireplace and push the big log through the door and onto the hearth to burn. The problem seemed to be that if you

123

were going to get a huge log like that to burn, then you would have to have a hot fire for it to lie on to start it off. But if you got the fire hot and then pushed the Yule log through the iron door, then you would only push the fire out onto the dining room carpet, which might not be the best idea. And you couldn't push the Yule log though just a bit, and then lift it onto the fire without burning your arms off.

Perdita thought it was an interesting problem. In the end it was agreed that what you would do would be to use Granny's kindling that she had been drying out in the AGA, and put the end of the Yule log on top of that, and put lots of little logs around it, and then you would light the kindling, and then bring a bucket of hot ashes from one of the other fires and put those around it so that it would all burn up and the Yule log would be in the middle of the flames and catch alight.

By the time they got back to the Grange, the wind was getting stronger and the snow was snowing quite hard, and the idea of a huge fire and Christmas lunch seemed a very good one, even to Jake. He had wanted to go out and play blizzards, but Aunty Cass had pointed out that it looked very much like a real blizzard, and real blizzards were not really something to be played in, whatever that nice Mr Ransome said. And so he decided that lighting the Yule log was going to be more fun. Which it was, but not quite in the way that he, or anybody else, expected it to be.

Chapter 11

Grandprof said: 'The Yule log is sometimes a birch log, and it's named after Juul which was the Scandinavian name of the winter solstice, and was a tribute the Norse god Thor. Tradition says that the person who lights it again has to have clean hands. Are your hands clean, Mike? And then the log is supposed to burn until Twelfth Night and you spread the ashes across the fields for fertiliser – apart from the ones you keep under the bed.' He was sitting at the dining room table with Perdita. Jake was helping Uncle Mike to move logs around the hearth and Daddy and Uncle Zac were outside in the snow, positioning the Yule log, so it just poked through the iron doorway into the back of the hearth.

When they got back from church, the grownups had made coffee, and Mummy and Granny and the Aunts had taken over the kitchen which suddenly became very warm and busy. Perdita stood quietly in a corner, watching, and then went to inspect the egg-boxes. Dulcie and Laura were playing Jenga in the playroom, and Josie was playing running up and down the landing and heading Max off from falling down the stairs.

Grandprof was sitting in the dining room.

'I could help, you know,' he said, as she came and sat beside him and watched the sticks and the logs and the Yule log being arranged, and Uncle Zac came in with a bucket of hot ashes and embers from the living room fire, and the sticks caught fire and the smoke started to wind its way up the huge chimney.

'But you're very old, Grandprof,' Perdita said. 'You don't have to help.'

'He's very lazy,' said Uncle Mike, and then Granny came in and said could they all be somewhere else because it was time to lay the table. And so while Aunty Fee and Aunty Rill were carrying glasses and plates and cutlery and crackers and place mats into the dining room, Daddy curled up in front of the playroom fire and they all piled up around him, and he read about Christmas Day in *A Christmas Carol*.

After all his adventures with the spirits of Christmas Past, Christmas Present, and Christmas Yet to Come, Scrooge wakes up, very pleased to be alive, and sorry that he had been such an old miser, and finds that he hasn't missed Christmas after all.

He was checked in his transports by the churches ringing out the lustiest peals he had ever heard. Clash, clang, hammer; ding, dong, bell. Bell, dong, ding; hammer, clang, clash! Oh, glorious, glorious!

Running to the window, he opened it, and put out his head. No fog, no mist; clear, bright, jovial, stirring, cold; cold, piping for the blood to dance to; Golden sunlight; Heavenly sky; sweet fresh air; merry bells. Oh, glorious! Glorious!

'What's today!' cried Scrooge, calling downward to a boy in Sunday clothes, who perhaps had loitered in to look about him.

'Eh?' returned the boy, with all his might of wonder.

'What's today, my fine fellow?' said Scrooge.

'Today!' replied the boy. 'Why, Christmas Day.'

'It's Christmas Day!' said Scrooge to himself. 'I haven't missed it. The Spirits have done it all in one night. They can do anything they like. Of course they can. Of course they can. Hallo, my fine fellow!'

'Hallo!' returned the boy.

'Do you know the Poulterer's, in the next street but one, at the corner?' Scrooge inquired.

'I should hope I did,' replied the lad.

'An intelligent boy!' said Scrooge. 'A remarkable boy! Do you know whether they've sold the prize Turkey that was hanging up there?—Not the little prize Turkey: the big one?'

'What, the one as big as me?' returned the boy.

'What a delightful boy!' said Scrooge. 'It's a pleasure to talk to him. Yes, my buck!'

'It's hanging there now,' replied the boy.

'Is it?' said Scrooge. 'Go and buy it.'

'Walk-er!' exclaimed the boy.

'No, no,' said Scrooge, 'I am in earnest. Go and buy it, and tell 'em to bring it here, that I may give them the direction where to take it. Come back with the man, and I'll give you a shilling. Come back with him in less than five minutes and I'll give you half-a-crown!'…

Scrooge was better than his word…. He became as good a friend, as good a master, and as good a man as the good old City knew, or any other good old city, town, or borough in the good old world. Some people laughed to see the alteration in him, but he let them laugh, and little heeded them; for he was wise enough to know that nothing ever happened on this globe, for good, at which some people did not have their fill of laughter in the outset; and, knowing that such as these would be blind anyway, he thought it quite as well that they should wrinkle up their eyes in grins as have the malady in less attractive forms. His own heart laughed: and that was quite enough for him.

He had no further intercourse with Spirits, but lived upon the Total-Abstinence Principle ever afterwards; and it was always said of him that he knew how to keep Christmas well, if any man alive possessed the knowledge. May that be truly said of us, and all of us! And so, as Tiny Tim observed, God bless Us, Every One!

So that was alright then. And then it was time for lunch.

On her way upstairs to wash her hands and brush her hair, Perdita looked into the dining room. The table was lovely – just like the pictures – lines of plates and knives and forks and crackers and glasses; wreaths of holly and ivy and berries, and every plate had a cracker on it. There were two high chairs – for Max and Laura. Perfect. The only thing was, that there was a haze in the room. She looked at the fire. It was blazing, as the books said it should, merrily, and the end of the big Yule log did seem to have caught fire. But, as she looked, a gust of snowy cold air blew in from the space around the log where it lay half in and half out of the iron doorway, and the smoke of the fire puffed out into the room, and a spatter of melted snow sprayed and flopped onto the carpet.

Behind her, Uncle Mike said, 'Uh-oh.'

Granny came along the hall carrying a tray with gravy and bread sauce and stuffing and roast potatoes on it. 'The only trouble with the dining room is that the kitchen is such a long way away,' she said. Perdita thought for a moment that Uncle Mike was going to try to stop her going into the dining room, but he stood aside. Granny took one step into the room, just as a big gust of wind hit the side of the house and rattled the windows, and huge whoosh of snow and steam and smoke and ashes flew up into the room. Bits of black settled on the white tablecloth.

So Christmas lunch was relocated to the kitchen. Perdita stood in the hall, Keeping Out Of The Way, and watched as Mummy and Granny took everything off the dining room table and put it into two washing baskets and took it all away to the kitchen, while Uncle Mike and Daddy went outside and pulled the Yule log, throwing off sparks, back out through the iron doorway. Inside, Uncle Zac danced in the hearth, poking at logs which smoked and glowed at him. Perdita tiptoed – in case Uncle Zac should think that she shouldn't be in the dining room – to the window so she could watch, although he was much too concerned about keeping the logs in the hearth without getting burned, and as the Yule log was pulled out, the wind and the snow swept in. Perdita had read about howling gales, and here was a real one. The snow was flying about the room and hissing on the fire.

Outside, Uncle Mike and Daddy had hauled the Yule log clear of the house, where it lay hissing in the snow, and then they shut the iron door with a clang and Uncle Mike pushed the outside bolt across. Jake had been standing in the snow, watching, in his indoor shoes and without a coat.

Perdita went back into the hall as they came back through front door with snow all over their clothes and black all over their faces and hands. Uncle Mike had one of his calm conversations with Jake, who ran upstairs. The fire in the dining room hearth, poked into discipline by Uncle Zac seemed to lose its enthusiasm and started to go out, but the smoke from it refused to go up the chimney. In the end, Uncle Zac simply shut the dining room door and let the smoke, which was trying to get into the hall, do whatever it liked.

~

Perdita, sorting it out later in her mind, was not sure what to make of Christmas lunch, dinner, or whatever it was. But it was pleasantly chaotic.

They began by having crackers, which made Laura cry and started an argument between Daddy and Josie as to who was going to have the purple paper hat. And then Uncle Mike carved the turkey, and Aunty Rill grew another four arms, and plates were passed, and parsnips and carrots and cauliflower cheese and roast potatoes and peas and stuffing and bread sauce and gravy spooned and ladled and, in some cases, thrown.

Laura had decided that the only edible things on the table were the roast potatoes and Aunty Fee had given up trying to persuade her to eat a pea. Dulcie had discovered bread sauce, and thought it was the Best Thing Ever, and wanted it on everything. Perdita who was by nature what Mummy called in her calmer moments a Conservative Eater, was delighted to find that she was sitting next to Grandprof who seemed to generate a sort of peaceful field around himself and was carefully eating only the things that he liked. These did not include vegetables (except roast potatoes), which Grandprof said were very bad for you unless you were a horse. So he and Perdita shared some breast of Turkey (even though, as Grandprof said, it had been described by somebody as tasting of a mixture of warmed up plaster of Paris and horsehair) and some of the stuffing that she had helped to make, and a lot of peas, which Grandprof said weren't really a vegetable.

'Pity we didn't catch a carp or two,' he said. 'One of those books in the library says that pies made of carps' tongues were all the rage at Christmas in Elizabethan times.'

Across the table, Jake heard this, and you could almost see another idea forming in his head.

When it came to the Christmas pudding, there was a vote about who liked it, and who liked it only because of the money that had been put in it. And those people (like Grandprof) who wouldn't eat it even if it had been made of 95% money. Then Mummy switched the lights off, and Aunty Rill poured brandy (not methylated spirits) over the pudding and lighted it and the blue flames wobbled – rather than danced – over it and around it, and she cut a slice and put it on a plate, and slid a spoonful of flames over it.

'Pity it tastes horrible,' Grandprof said, but Perdita tried some, and it was alright, but she had a small apple pie with cream instead.

~

The meal really ended when the littles had had enough and were put down on the floor, and then Perdita and Sebastian and Dulcie and Jake and Josie got their coats and boots on and Uncle Mike (with Max on his shoulders) and Uncle Zac and Aunty Rill went with them. It was still windy and snowing hard, so they went round to the stableyard and Daddy found a washing-line and they roped themselves together with it and went for an expedition. They took turns to be lowered down the ha-ha, and swung across the stream by the old mill ruins, and they slipped and slithered along the edge of the carp ponds. Perdita wondered if the fishes could see it snowing. Looking back, they could hardly see the house through the dusk and the falling snow and then they had another snowball fight and went indoors.

~

Perdita rather liked taking her boots off and putting warm socks on and a sweater that wasn't damp around the shoulders. The kitchen was full of steaminess, and they had a hot lemony drink that Aunty Cass had made, and then it was time for the play. In her bedroom, Mummy had laid out the costumes, which were really their dressing-gowns with some extra things, and they got dressed up and went downstairs.

Dulcie was allowed to bang the tea tray until everybody was ready and they all went into the playroom, where there was a fire made of red wrapping paper in the middle of the floor and the sofas had been moved around so that everyone could see what was happening. Grandprof sat in a corner with the script.

There was a lot of scuffling around, and Perdita and Sebastian, in their dressing-gowns and carrying long sticks for crooks, and Dulcie's lamb, came out from behind the sofa, and sat by the paper fire. Laura and Max both with white woolly ears came and sat behind them. After a moment, Laura changed her mind about this, and went and sat on Aunty Fee, and Max decided to see if he could sit on the fire and was retrieved by Aunty Cass and placed firmly on her knee.

Jake, in his dressing gown, but with a big carrier bag in his hand, stood up.

'Welcome to our play,' he said. 'Written by Grandprof. Has everybody got a programme?'

The programme said:

The Shepherds' Play

Characters
Shepherd 1 – Perdita
Shepherd 2 – Sebastian
Mack – Jake
Mack's Wife – Josie

Angel – Dulcie
Sheep – Laura and Max

And some of them had sheep and stars drawn on them, and some had mysterious things that Dulcie had drawn.

'The first scene,' Jake said, 'is the hill above Bethlehem, and the Shepherds are watching over their flocks by night.'

And the play went like this:

PERDITA: Gosh it's cold.

SEBASTIAN: I think it's going to snow.

PERDITA: It's not fair, the way we have to stay out on the hillside with our sheep, when everyone else is down in the village, all warm and cosy.

SEBASTIAN: And I think it's going to snow. It's in the air.

PERDITA: And there's something else going on. I heard that three strangers have been asking where they can find a new baby. I don't know, do you?

SEBASTIAN: No. And I think it's going to snow.

PERDITA: Look there's somebody coming. Oh, no. It's Mack, the sheep-stealer. We'd better keep a close eye on our sheep!

Jake came on, looking very fierce.

JAKE: Good evening, shepherds! It's a cold night, isn't it.

SEBASTIAN: I think it's going to snow.

PERDITA: What do you want, Mack? Don't think you're going to steal any of our sheep. We're too clever for you.

JAKE : I wouldn't dream of such a thing. I was just thinking of you up here on the hills, and how cold you must be, so I've bought you a hot drink.

SEBASTIAN: That's not like you, Mack.

JAKE: Well, I was down in the village just now, and I passed a man and a woman with a donkey, and they were looking for somewhere to sleep. There was no room at the inn, but the innkeeper let them stay in his stable. The innkeeper's wife brought them hot drinks, and she was so kind that I thought I should be kind too.

PERDITA: You did, did you?

JAKE: So here I am, and here are the hot drinks.

PERDITA: Well … it is a very cold night.

SEBASTIAN: I think it's going to snow. I'd like a hot drink. Thank you.

JAKE: Would you like some? Go on.

PERDITA: Oh, very well. (Perdita yawned a huge yawn.) What sort of drink is it?

JAKE: Just a sleeping potion. Goodnight!

Perdita and Sebastian yawned a lot more and then stretched and lay down on the carpet and went to sleep.

JAKE: That should keep them quiet! Now, I fancy roast lamb for supper!

He grabbed Dulcie's lamb and went round the back of the sofa. And after a pause and a slight scuffle, Dulcie bounced out wearing a very tight while sparkly dress and with a big star on the end of a bamboo stick. She was concentrating very hard, and got all her words out in the right order.

DULCIE: Wake up! Wake up! Come on, wake up! You must go down to Bethlehem to find the baby Jesus. You will find him lying in a manger. And someone has stolen one of your lambs.

PERDITA: It must have been that villain Mack! Let's go to Bethlehem and get our lamb back.

SEBASTIAN: And then we'll find the baby Jesus. But I think it's going to snow.

They got up, and Jake came back in and took the fire away, and then Perdita and Sebastian carried the crib in and placed it in the middle of the floor, and went away again and hid. Josie came in, holding Dulcie's lamb, followed by Jake, who stood for a moment as if he were going to say something, and then turned to the audience and said: 'The scene changes to Mack's house. And this is Mrs Mack.'

JOSIE: This is a lovely lamb. What shall we do with it? I like roast lamb. Or lamb stew perhaps?

JAKE: I don't mind. I'll just take it outside and kill it!

There was a booing from the audience, and Perdita and Sebastian called from behind the sofa.

PERDITA: Mack! Mack! Where are you?

SEBASTIAN: We want our lamb back before it snows.

JOSIE: What shall we do? I know! I'll wrap it in this shawl and put it in the cradle. Now, lamb, lie there and be quiet!

Josie put the lamb in the cradle and tucked it in neatly, and Perdita and Sebastian entered, dramatically.

PERDITA: OK, Mack! Where's our the lamb?

JAKE: I don't know what you're talking about.

JOSIE: There's no lamb here. You can search the house if you like.

Sebastian and Perdita made such a good job of searching, that Jake obviously felt bound to speed things along a little, and said 'Baaaaa'.

PERDITA: What's in that cradle?

JOSIE: My baby of course. He's got a bit of a cold. That's why he's going 'baa'.

PERDITA: Oh, poor baby! Let me give him a cuddle.

She dramatically threw the cot blanket aside and pulled out the lamb by its ears.

JOSIE: Oh dear! My baby's turned into a lamb!

There was a good deal of laughing from the audience, and Dulcie bounced on again.

DULCIE: Now peace to everyone. There is a real baby next door in the stable, and he would love to see the lamb.

PERDITA: That would be lovely. We can give him the lamb as a present.

JAKE: We'll come too!

JOSIE: It's going to be a wonderful night.

SEBASTIAN: If it doesn't snow.

They all came to the front and bowed, and everyone clapped, and Perdita, watching them carefully, decided that they were all clapping because they meant it, and not be *patronising*,

'That was a bit irreverent wasn't it?' said Aunty Cass to Grandprof, who was looking very pleased.

'Don't blame me,' Grandprof said. 'It's based on the *Second Shepherds' Pageant* sometime from around 1450. Performed at York by the Chandlers, at Chester by the Painters and Glaziers, and at Coventry by the Shearmen and Tailors.'

Aunty Cass gave him a look which Perdita thought, she might have given to her own Daddy.

'Well done the Shearman,' she said.

Chapter 12

In Which Perdita Remembers her Key and There is a Bedtime Story

And then it was present time.

Perdita sat on Daddy's foot, because it seemed a good place to sit, and Uncle Zac, who was obviously now the fire monitor, put some more logs on the living room fire, and Mummy and Aunty Cass took charge of distributing the presents. In a very few minutes, the world, Perdita thought, almost disappeared into a snowstorm of wrapping paper. She had a huge flat paint box from Mummy and Daddy, and Jake had a remote-controlled electric model car, which he immediately started to race up and down the hall, and Josie had a new leotard and ballet skirt and shoes and went off straight away into the playroom to change into them. Sebastian – and Perdita could tell that he was very very pleased by the fact that he was very very quiet – unwrapped some very old maps that Grandprof had bought him, and went and sat on the stairs, opening each fold very carefully, as if he were opening magic boxes, which perhaps he was.

Then Daddy started to play more carols, and they sang 'In the Bleak Midwinter', which was very appropriate, and Perdita went to the window that looked out over the lawn, and all she could see was the patch of snow where the light from the window fell.

'Snow had fallen, snow on snow.
Snow on snow…'

And it really had.

Then they sang 'Hey Little Bull' again, because everyone liked it, and 'The Colours of Mary' because it had such a sad tune.

Perdita went into the kitchen and helped Aunty Rill finish the washing up, and Aunty Rill made her a ham sandwich, and Christmas Day drifted pleasantly away, with complicated board games with Daddy on the living room floor, and playing jumping off the sofas with Max and Dulcie, and watching Aunty Rill and Daddy playing an endless game of skittles, which was fun because she helped to take the balls back and put the skittles up again when they'd been knocked down. The balls rumbled on the wooden alley, and hit the pins with a sharp click and rattle, and then thumped into the blanket that was hanging from the wall. All very satisfactory.

At one point, she went back up the cellar steps and through the kitchen, opened the dining room door, and switched on the light. The curtains were open, and with the cold white and black outdoors, the room looked desolate. And very dirty. The fire had burned down to a dull glow, but there was ash everywhere. She was about to close the door and pretend she hadn't seen it, when she saw the purse lying on the top of the cabinet. Perhaps nobody had seen it because everyone had been so busy. She walked lightly across the room, and picked it up, and slipped it into the pocket of her skirt.

~

'I thought we should have a Christmassy story,' Daddy said.

'Sounds like an idea,' Mummy said.

There was a good deal of snuggling around the fire. Aunty Fee was feeding the baby, and Laura was in bed (with a baby alarm plugged in to her bedroom, although she never waked), and Max was half asleep on Uncle Mike's chest, his batteries run down at last, Perdita thought. She resisted the temptation to reach out and stroke his head.

'It's two stories really,' Daddy said, 'and Sebastian put me on to it.'

'It's on one of the maps that Grandprof gave me,' Sebastian said. 'It's a legend about the farm just up the lane, which is a very unusual place, because it was built on top of an old British earthwork that was thousands of years old. Right in the middle. The place is a bit like our Tump at home, but much much bigger and much more mysterious.' He stopped, looking rather surprised to have said quite o much.

Jake, who was sitting in his usual place on the back of the bigger sofa, said, 'Yes, I read a book about earthworks. Nobody knows how they managed to build them. They didn't have any diggers, and they've got great ditches all around and they're flat at the top.'

'Absolutely,' Daddy said, 'and they were very holy places – like Stonehenge where people believed that great magics happened, and paths and tracks from all over the universe – not just the country – converged. So they were magic places and people were very careful not to disturb the magic by building on them – but the farm up the lane is a rare exception.

'Now, the earthworks had their fair share of stories told about them, but the most strange was the legend of the horses that didn't leave any footprints. For hundreds of years, people passing by the earthworks – especially around Christmas – would come down to the village saying that they had heard horses galloping across the tumulus, the earthworks, in the dark, but when they went the next day – and sometimes they took a priest – because they were so frightened – there were never any hoofprints. And it didn't matter whether it had been raining and the ground was soft. There were never any hoofprints.'

'Did anybody see the horses?' said Aunty Fee.

'Some people said they did, and some people thought they did, but most people just heard the hooves thumping. Well, of course, nobody likes living close to places where there are strange horse noises in the night, so the people around here – and this was long before our Grange was built – the people round here all moved away and went to live in the village. Woods grew up around the earthworks, and travellers sometimes said they could hear horses in the woods, even though there was no road for them to gallop on.'

Perdita looked up, hearing an echo in her head.

'OK,' Daddy said. 'That's one end of the story. Let's go back to the other end, and that's in Bethlehem, with the shepherds and the angels and the Baby Jesus in the manger. Now the thing that nobody asks is – who was using the manger before the Baby Jesus was laid in it? Just think: the inn was full, and it was full because people had come a long way to the census: and they all came on donkeys or horses or camels, so it was not just the inn that would have been full, but the stables and barns would have been bursting too – so, how was it that Mary and Joseph found a place in a stable? Doesn't make sense.'

They thought about this.

'It might have been the innkeeper's *private* stable,' Granny said.

'Well, it might,' Daddy said, 'but the simple answer is that when Mary and Joseph arrived, somebody had to be moved *out* of the stable – and of course it was one of the horses that had to move out to make room. The donkeys were very tough and would probably have been tied up outside, and the camels would probably have been put in a barn, or kept by peoples' tents. And the sheep were up on the hills.'

'What about the cows?' Sebastian said. 'The hymn says, "born in a cattle stall"'.

'Well that just shows how much hymn writers know,' Daddy said. 'The cows wouldn't have been in the stable in the first place. They would have been in a cowshed, and a cattle stall would be where they brought the cattle in to milk them.'

'So it would have been empty,' Sebastian said, 'if the cattle weren't being milked.'

Daddy looked at him. 'Well, that's true, but the *story* says that it was a stable and not a cowshed, and so it was a horse that had to gave up her stall to Mary and Joseph. The legend is that the horse that was moved out was called Grey Mary or Mari Lwyd, and it was particularly nice of her because she had only recently had a foal herself, and the foal was turned out as well.

'Of course the horse didn't mind giving up the manger and stall for Mary and Joseph and the Baby Jesus when he arrived, and she was able to put her head over the side of the stall, along with the cows and donkeys (the donkeys had to stand on straw bales because they weren't tall enough) and to see the baby and watch what was going on. But it was all so engrossing, and the baby was so interesting and *holy* and all, that she quite forgot about her foal.'

'Awww,' said Dulcie.

'Quite right,' Daddy said. 'And that was why when everything had calmed down and the angels had stopped singing and the shepherds had gone back to their sheep – the three wise men didn't turn up for another few days – and the baby had settled down for the night, Grey Mary suddenly remembered her foal, and went to look for her. But she couldn't find her anywhere. So she wandered over the hills, looking and looking and neighing, and wondering where her foal could have got to.

'Now it seems that while she as looking at the baby Jesus, her foal was feeling rather sad and lost, and so the friendly spirits of the night, who are a lot like angels, gathered her up into their arms, so she could trot around the stars. And those spirits watched Grey Mary searching and getting sadder and sadder until when they had thought she had been sad for long enough, they took pity on her, and swept her up into the sky to be with her foal.

'Ever since then, when it comes to Christmas, Grey Mary and her foal gallop all over the world, visiting all the holy places – not big cathedrals or temples or churches, but humble places in the country. Some people think that Grey Mary wants to show her foal the Baby Jesus: some people think that it's an eternal punishment for neglecting her foal: and some say that in fact she and her foal do find the Baby Jesus at every holy place they go to, only we can't see him.

'So you can see that the earthworks just up the valley were just the sort of place that they would come down to and gallop around – and, of course, because they were magic horses, they never left any hoofprints.

'Ahh,' said Perdita.

'But that's not the whole story,' Daddy said. 'It's not the best bit.' He paused. '*This* bit is about a Blacksmith, but he wasn't a BAD Blacksmith like some of the Blacksmiths in stories. He was a very GOOD Blacksmith. He was kind to everyone, and he was popular wherever he went. You see, in those days, horses were everywhere, and every village had a Blacksmith – sometimes two. But the very little hamlets and remote farms didn't have one, and so some Blacksmiths were itinerants – that means that they travelled from farm to farm and hamlet to hamlet and shoed horses and mended things.

'Now, as I say, our Blacksmith was very popular, and one reason was that he often shoed horses for nothing, if the person who owned the horse was very poor. And as he travelled around, he would often give whatever food he had to anyone who was hungry. The result of this was that he (and his horse – because he carried his anvil and his tools and his crimps and his nails on a little cart) were often hungry themselves. But he didn't mind – although he was sorry for his horse sometimes – as long as he was making other people happy.

'So, one day, just before Christmas, he had been shoeing some horses at a farm higher up the valley, and was on his way to Tolpuddle where he was going to spend Christmas with his old mother – when it suddenly started to snow. And you know how hard it can snow around here! And it snowed and it snowed and it snowed, and the poor Blacksmith and his horse got completely lost, and the snow was so deep that they couldn't pull the cart through it.

'They came to a place where the ground rose steeply and they had to stop. Of course, it was actually the sides of the ancient earthworks, where nobody ever went, but they had no choice but to stop. So the Blacksmith wrapped the horse up in a blanket, and gave him some hay – which they carried on the cart as well – and lit a little fire under the cart – because of course he always carried kindling, and huddled up as warm as he could get.

'He was just dozing off, when his horse whinnied, and he woke up and looked out from under the cart, and there above them galloping through the sky, were Grey Mary and her foal. They circled round and landed on the snow, and came to a halt. He wasn't a bit afraid – remember he had been working with horses for years and years and years – so he stood up and went to meet them.

'The foal was limping, and Grey Mary said to the Blacksmith – and remember that he had been working with horses for years and years and years and understood everything they said – she said, "Master Smith, my foal is limping after all these many miles. Can you help us?" and the Blacksmith went and blew up his fire, and got his tools, and he shod the foal, and reshod Grey Mary, whose feet were very worn too, and they were very pleased.

'And Grey Mary said, "And how can we repay you, Master Smith?" and the Blacksmith said "I need no payment. I am just happy to see that you are well shod." And Grey Mary said, "You are a very good man, and so I shall give you some very good advice. Always trust your dreams!" and she and her foal leapt into the air on their new shoes and galloped away.

'Well, the Blacksmith thought he must have been dreaming, but there were his tools all hot from the fire, so he shook his head and lay down to sleep again.

'But almost at once he had a dream, and it was Grey Mary, and she said to him, "You must go to Stonehenge at once, and hear what you will hear!"

'And then he woke up, and told his horse what he had dreamed, and the horse said, "Well, we'd better get going! Remember what Grey Mary said! Trust your dreams!"

'So they packed up their camp and set off through the snow towards Stonehenge. It took them a couple of days to get there, and when they got there, they looked around, but the place was deserted – only the great grey stones standing in a circle. Two days before, and the place would have been crowded with worshippers who had come to celebrate the Winter Solstice because it was a really holy place, but everyone who had come for the solstice had already gone away again. There was nobody there but one old man whose job was to clear up all the rubbish and the litter that people had left behind.

'So the Blacksmith stopped his cart, and sat on it, and waited for something to happen. But nothing did. So he went and asked the old man if he would like some help with clearing up, and the old man was very grim and gruff and said "Please yourself.!" Now, as you know, the Blacksmith was a very good man, and so he pleased himself by working hard all day, picking up rubbish in a sack and putting it on a great big pile. The old man had a little hut with a fire going outside it, and every hour he would stop for tea and get warm, but he never asked the Blacksmith to join him, or offered him any tea, or gave him a friendly word.

'When it got to the end of the day, the old man shut up his hut and went home, and the Blacksmith camped under his cart and had a very cold night, wondering all the time why Grey Mary in his dream had told him to come to Stonehenge. She had said to trust his dream, and he had, but nothing had happened.

The next morning it was Christmas Eve, and the old man came back and lit the fire and made himself a cup of tea. Then he looked at the Blacksmith, who was sitting on his cart, and said, "Tell me, Blacksmith. What are you doing here? What are you sitting there for?"

'And the Blacksmith told him about the dream, and how he'd been told to go to Stonehenge and to hear what he should hear.

'Then the old man laughed and said, "More fool you! You must be very simple-minded to listen to dreams. Why I had a dream the other night, and this voice said to me that I should go to Tolpuddle as fast as I could, and dig in some tumulus or other, and I'd find a pot of gold!" He sneered. "What a load of nonsense. You won't catch me going on a wild goose chase like that, just because of a stupid dream!"

'But by then he was talking to himself because the Blacksmith had jumped onto his cart and was driving as fast as he could back to Tolpuddle, and up the lane to the earthworks.

'It was the middle of Christmas Day by the time he arrived and he and his horse were exhausted, but they drove into the earthwork, and there in the very middle was a patch of snow that had melted. So the Blacksmith stopped his cart (and fed his horse, of course) and got his spade, and ran to the very middle of the earthwork, where the snow had melted, and dug and dug. And before long, his spade hit something hard, and he dug and dug – and he found a great urn, and it was full to the brim with gold coins!

'And do you know what he did? He built a brand new farm on that very spot, and it had lots of stables, and he took in all the old and broken down horses from miles and miles around and gave them happy homes. And he gave lots of money to all the poor people – because the money never seemed to run out. And every year he celebrated Christmas and had all the poor people from the villages and farms all around for a great feast. And while they were eating, he would go and stand in his stable yard, and heat up his forge, and every year he would shoe Grey Mary and her foal so that they could gallop around the skies for ever.'

~

After Dulcie was asleep, Sebastian brought one of his maps over to Perdita's bed.

'That's quite true,' he said. 'The bit about the farm being built on a prehistoric earthwork. And there was a road once, from the mill and down through the woods. But it's gradually disappeared.' They looked at the map together, and the faint lines, and Perdita nodded, and Sebastian went back to bed.

Perdita switched off her bedside light, and lay looking at the pale light of the snow reflected on the ceiling. Then she felt for her torch, and found the right book in the pile beside her bed, and took it under the duvet, and found the right poem.

> They shut the road through the woods
> Seventy years ago.
> Weather and rain have undone it again,
> And now you would never know
> There was once a road through the woods
> Before they planted the trees.
> It is underneath the coppice and heath,
> And the thin anemones.
> Only the keeper sees
> That, where the ring-dove broods,
> And the badgers roll at ease,
> There was once a road through the woods.
>
> Yet, if you enter the woods
> Of a summer evening late,
> When the night-air cools on the trout-ringed pools
> Where the otter whistles his mate,
> (They fear not men in the woods,

Because they see so few.)
You will hear the beat of a horse's feet,
And the swish of a skirt in the dew,
Steadily cantering through
The misty solitudes,
As though they perfectly knew
The old lost road through the woods.
But there is no road through the woods.

And she went to sleep, wondering.

26 DECEMBER

BOXING DAY

Chapter 13

In Which Some Things are Not What they Seem

Grandprof put down the book he had been reading and stretched his legs out in front of the fire. 'How's Boxing Day been so far?'

Perdita leaned back against the back of the sofa. The answer was, of course, very good.

The day had begun almost before it was light, with Jake and Josie and Sebastian having a snowball fight outside her window. Perdita and Dulcie went down to join in, and they decided to build an igloo, which was not a great success because it turned out that you needed lots and lots and *lots* of big snowballs to build even the smallest igloo – and they didn't have a shed to start with. So they turned it into a Viking ship and were battling snow monsters when Granny came out to call them in for breakfast.

Jake and Josie had taken snowballs up to Aunty Rill's room and had got very wet when they pushed open her bedroom door and a washing-up bowl of water which Aunty Rill had balanced on top of it fell on their heads. The only person who didn't find this entirely funny had been Aunty Cass, who had to provide dry clothes, although she said she didn't really see why she should, and it wasn't her fault that she belonged to a family of idiots.

Breakfast was a lot of fried ham, which Aunty Rill said was worth getting up for, and then Granny and Mummy and Daddy seemed to be spending the morning spring-cleaning the dining room, and there were so many games being played and so much running around that after a while Perdita had looked for somewhere quiet, and that was sitting on the sofa with Grandprof.

Mummy put her head round the door. 'I've just had a phone call from the Vicar and she says that the two old ladies at High Puddle Farm would love a visit if we'd like to go for morning coffee. Coming?'

And so it was that half an hour later, four figures waded their way through the snow down the drive to the lane. There was Mummy, and Perdita, and Sebastian, who wanted to see what the farm was like and what the earthworks were like, and Josie, who had heard the story of *Little Women* too, and thought that she would be the perfect Beth. There had been something of a debate about what to take, and in the end they thought that a big flask of soup for the old ladies' lunch, and a loaf of bread that Granny had made that morning, and a packet of chocolate biscuits for elevenses. After even more debate, Jake donated a large Toblerone, and Uncle Zac donated a box of Maltesers. And then Aunty Cass said that really there was too much turkey left, so they cut off the remaining leg and wrapped it in foil. All these goodies were packed into Mummy's rucksack, except for the Toblerone and the Maltesers, which were in Perdita's rucksack.

When they got to the lane, the first thing they saw was that a tractor – to judge by the huge tracks – had been up and down it, which made it much easier to walk on, but dented slightly the idea that they were visiting isolated old ladies, if they had already been visited by tractors. But Perdita had in her head a very clear image of two frail old things, dressed in velvet with white lace caps, sitting around the remains of a fire, their frail hands clutching bowls of tea, while the icy wind blew in under the parlour door. Soup and turkey and chocolate biscuits would save them from starving. She was wondering whether they should have brought some sticks for their fire.

The track ran along the side of the wood, crossed a bridge over the millstream, and then went up a slope into a very large farmyard. There were low buildings along three sides, and the tractor, steaming slightly, was standing by an open barn. Sebastian, who had been looking at the tracks in the snow, said, with some surprise, 'It must live here.' There was a car, too, deeply buried in snow, and bootprints crossing and re-crossing the yard. On the fourth side was a neat thatched cottage, and somebody in a large brown waxed jacket was stamping its boots free from snow, in the porch.

Mummy said, 'Hello?' and the figure turned, and pushed back its hood. It had a lot of grey hair, wound up into a sort of bun, and a tanned face.

'Ah, you're our visitors from the Grange,' the woman said. 'How nice of you to come. Come in and welcome!' and they followed her into the cottage. They were in a hallway with a red brick floor: to their left was a living room, with a bright wood fire burning, and to the right a step down into a long low kitchen. And it was a warm kitchen, with low beams, decorated by strings of Christmas cards. Another old lady, dressed in a heavy sweater and brown corduroy trousers, and with a large apron on, was stirring a large pan on the top of the AGA. On a rack behind the AGA were stacks of shining steel cans. There were low cupboards along the wall, and on their tops were the remains of a large turkey – larger than the one back at the Grange, plates of mince pies, and a pile of foil-covered balls, a little larger than cricket balls. And a ham, loosely covered with baking paper, and a pile of loaves of crusty bread.

'Come in, come you in,' said the second old lady cheerfully. 'I'm Martha, and this is my sister Susan. You're from the Grange, the Vicar says. I hope you're comfortable there.'

Mummy, who seemed to be having as much trouble reconciling what she was seeing with what she had expected to see as Perdita was, said 'Yes, yes, we are,' and introduced Perdita and Sebastian and Josie.

'Well, you're just in time for coffee. Or would you prefer hot chocolate?' Martha said, and she arranged them at the wooden kitchen table – it was big enough to seat six, and put a big pan on the AGA boiling plate and poured milk out of a tall can. There was a huge tin of hot chocolate powder, and she ladled four heaped spoonfuls into the pan, and then four big spoonfuls of sugar from a stone jar. She caught Josie looking at her with her eyes wide.

'I think there's never enough sugar, don't you?' she said, and stirred the mixture.

Josie wasn't the only one with wide eyes. Mummy was clearly trying to think of something to say, while Perdita's picture of the cold and old and lonely had evaporated.

Susan, having taken off her boots and put on floppy woolly slippers, came over to the AGA, and opened the bottom oven door, and brought out a pan of chocolate brownies and slid them onto the table.

'The Vicar,' Mummy said, with her eyes on the brownies, 'said she was worried that you didn't make it to church.'

'Yes, she said,' said Susan. 'Very nice of her, but there was no need. We couldn't get the car out on Christmas eve what with the snow, and on Christmas morning we had trouble with the tractor. Water pump seized up, of all things. It took me most of the morning to fix it, and then we were behind with deliveries.' She poured coffee for Mummy and Susie.

'Deliveries?' Mummy said faintly. Susie was cutting chocolate brownies and putting them onto plates. They were, Perdita thought, the Best Kind of brownies, slightly crisp on the outside and gooey in the middle.

Susan looked at Sebastian, who was contemplating the turkey. 'You're thinking it's a bit big for the two of us? Well, it would be. But we do Christmas dinners for anyone who's on their own or not very well off. We generally do soup as well.' Martha poured mugs of hot chocolate and set them in front of Perdita and Sebastian and Josie, and poured coffee for Mummy.

'Susan's just back from a delivery run,' Martha said. 'And the soup's ready, so we're about to load up and do another round.'

Sebastian said, with considerable respect. 'Do *you* drive that tractor?'

Susan looked at him. 'And why shouldn't I, young man?'

Perdita looked at Sebastian. He said, brightly, 'Well, it looks very heavy. Does it have power steering?'

Susan laughed. 'Very good. Actually, it does, of sorts. I thought you were going to say that you thought I was too old.'

'How old are you?' said Josie.

'If you must know,' Susan said, 'I'm eighty-eight and young Martha there's eighty-seven. Not too old to drive tractors.'

'Do you live here on your own?' Mummy said, keeping her voice, Perdita thought, very level, so that she wasn't implying that there would be any reason why they shouldn't.

'Oh, yes,' Martha said. 'These thirty years. But we have our grandson, George, staying with us over Christmas. He's tending to the cow at the moment. We keep just one cow. That's more than enough for us.' She took some of the cans from the rack, and began filling them with soup.

'You won't be seeing him, though,' Susan said. She still hadn't sat down, and was holding her hands around her coffee mug. 'He's very shy.'

'It's a sad story,' Martha said. 'He had an accident when he was about ten, and it scarred his face quite badly. And now he's a teenager he hates seeing people, or he hates people seeing him, and it's particularly bad for him around Christmas what with the parties and everything. So for the last past few years he's been staying here over Christmas. He's a great help. He generally gets us a carp for Boxing Day from the Colonel's ponds. They're very good.'

Perdita felt as if she were living in a very old sort of novel, where boys had accidents, and they kept out of the way so nobody ever saw them, but they turned out to be really nice in the end.

Susan finished her coffee, pulled an empty crate out from under the table, and began to load it with cans of soup.

'We'll get out of your way,' Mummy said. 'Thank you very much for the coffee and the brownies.' Sebastian and Perdita, well trained, said the same. Josie thought for a minute and said, 'They were the *best* brownies I've ever had in my life!'

'Delighted you could come,' Martha said. 'Now, are you alright for provisions. We've got some turkey spare – or would you like some soup? Or a loaf of bread? You must have a lot of mouths to feed.'

'No, no, I think we're alright, thank you,' Mummy said. She put her backpack on, obviously hoping that it was invisible.

Perdita was opening *her* backpack. 'We brought you some chocolate,' she said, holding out the Toblerone and the Maltesers. 'Just for Christmas.'

'Well, you are angel-kinder,' Martha said. 'You have a kind heart. Thank you. Those are our favourites.'

When they were back in the farmyard, and Susan was tying the crate onto the back of the tractor, Sebastian said, 'Can I ask you something about the farm?'

Susan nodded. 'It's not really a farm any more. This stableyard was once very important, and the big old original farmhouse itself was over there. But times change, and farms get bigger and need fewer people, so most of this just went derelict, and they pulled the old farmhouse down. This yard is just an outpost now.'

'But is it really built on a tumulus?' Sebastian said.

Susan looked at him with a certain respect, as people did with Sebastian. 'It's built on a very ancient earthwork, if not exactly a tumulus. You can follow the ditches all the way round the back of the yard.' She followed his look. 'But we've never found any gold.' She finished tying the crate. 'The only other place like this we know of is over at Knowlton– there's a church there that was built in the centre of a Neolithic henge. Probably that's why it's haunted.' She climbed onto the tractor and turned the key. It shuddered into life, and with a neat click of the gears, and quite a lot of diesel fumes, bounced out of the gate, slid sideways, and disappeared down the lane.

'I have to say,' Martha said – she had been standing by the door, listening – 'that sometimes I think I hear hoofbeats in the night, but that's just the night for you. Now, are you sure there's nothing you need.'

'That's very kind,' Mummy said, 'but our cooks have worked out what they need down to the last mouthful,' and they all thanked her again, and went out of the farmyard, sliding on the tractor tracks.

Nobody said anything on the way back. Perdita didn't know what Josie was thinking (she was playing hitting the lower branches of the trees with a stick, and dodging the showers of snow), but she knew that Mummy and Sebastian were thinking about what was in Mummy's backpack, and were very glad that the poor starving old sisters hadn't asked.

Chapter 14

In Which Jake Lands a Fish, and Dulcie Lands on her Feet

When they got back to the house, and Mummy had quietly taken her backpack into the kitchen and quietly put the things in it back where they came from, they went out onto the front lawn to see where everyone was. It seemed that Grandprof had achieved a lifelong ambition and had made a snow car, and it was so successful that he had made two more smaller ones for Dulcie and Laura, and then he'd been sent up to have a bath by Granny, who said that he'd freeze to death if he didn't, and there wasn't room in the freezer at home to keep him so he better hadn't. You could see, Perdita thought, looking at Josie as Granny went indoors, that Josie had suddenly got quite a new idea about what Granny was like.

And then there was lots of shouting from the ponds, and Jake came running across the lawn carrying a fish. True, it was a small fish, not a lot bigger than Uncle Mike's hand, but it was a fish. Uncle Mike and Jake and Dulcie had gone for a voyage in the dinghy on the ponds – the only good bit of which had been pushing the dinghy into the water across the snow – it had slid off the bank very quickly and Uncle Mike was only just in time to catch the stern before it floated out of reach, and he very nearly fell in. So they sat and fished and nothing happened, but just when they were about to give up, Jake's float had bobbed and he'd pulled out the fish.

Sebastian dashed off to the library and came back with a fishing encyclopedia. The fish was lying on the kitchen table looking, Perdita thought, rather dead. Jake and Sebastian turned the pages and decided in the end that it was a Dace.

'A Common Dace,' Sebastian said.

'Common?' said Grandprof. 'Nothing common about that. Jake's first fish.'

'Also known as a Mud Carp,' Sebastian said. 'Part of the Cyprinidae family.'

'Quite the knobs, then,' Grandprof said.

Perdita looked at him.

'So it's a kind of carp,' Jake said. 'Can we have it for lunch?

'"Not highly regarded as a food fish"' Sebastian read, a touch remorselessly, Perdita thought. '"It is troublesome to eat because of the number of small spines."'

Jake looked disappointed, but Aunty Rill said – 'Don't worry. We can make a fish ball put of it without any bones,' and she proceeded to gut the Dace, under the cold tap, scraping the insides into the sink. Then she cut off its head, and put the body into a pan of water on the AGA. By that point, most of the watchers had quietly gone off to do something else, but Perdita and Jake loyally watched as the fish was boiled, and then Aunty Rill took it out of the pan and deftly stripped the soft flesh off the tiny bones. There didn't seem to be much.

'Now you have to chop it until it goes all sticky,' Aunty Rill said. She handed Jake a small knife. 'But don't get any blood in it. Ruins the colour.' She turned to Perdita. 'I'm doing fried sandwiches for lunch: mostly ham and cheese, but I know what you're like, so give me your order now.'

And so when Jake had done some enthusiastic banging with the ladle, and they all came back into the kitchen, there were fried sandwiches oozing cheese, and turkey sandwiches with cranberry sauce – and one for Perdita, which consisted of a slice of bread topped with strawberry jam, a slice of cheese, some chutney, some chopped bacon, another slice of cheese, and then another slice of bread. Perdita also wanted a slice of banana on top, but Aunty Rill said that there were limits, whatever that meant.

But the centrepiece of the meal was the fish ball which sat in the middle of the table on a dish of its own, and Sebastian and Uncle Mike were allowed to taste a very tiny bit because they had worked almost as hard for it, and then Josie and Dulcie had to try a little bit – but after that Aunty Rill said that Jake should have the rest. Jake had chopped the fish very finely, and Aunty Rill had shown him how to crack an egg and separate the white from the yolk. Then he had mixed the egg white with the fish and squeezed it into a ball. Then he had filled a pan with water and when it was boiling he dropped the ball into it.

'That's very good,' Aunty Rill said. 'They often fall apart. Must be very superior fish.'

'Let's go and catch another,' Jake said.

But he didn't get a chance until quite a lot later, because after lunch there was a lot of clearing up, and

Grandprof sat by the Library fire and read out bits from books about local ghosts.

'It says here, that not far away there's the most haunted house in Dorset. It's got a lady who walks through walls, and an ape that's scraping the walls of a secret passage that it got stuck in hundreds of years ago, a mysterious hooded priest, two swordsmen, a ghostly cooper in the cellar – that's a man who makes barrels – a lady who just says hello – she doesn't sound very exciting – a soldier from the first world war – although it doesn't say what he does, and a bride in the garden.'

'Sounds a bit overcrowded to me,' Mummy said.

'But I haven't found anything about a single ghost in this house,' Grandprof said.

'Very disappointing,' Mummy said. 'But now's your chance. We're going to play hide and seek.'

This seemed to Perdita to be a VERY good idea, even when Granny said that they had to play it in pairs. Grandprof was 'It' and Granny had Things to Look After in the AGA, and Aunty Fee was feeding the baby, and Perdita found herself paired with Uncle Zac and Laura – who counted as one, which was nice. They started in the hall, and the other pairs – Aunty Rill and Jake, Uncle Mike and Max, Aunty Cass and Josie, Daddy and Dulcie, and Mummy and Sebastian, set off along the corridor and up the stairs. Uncle Zac tugged Perdita by the arm and they went into the living room and hid behind the big sofa. Uncle Zac pulled it a little closer to the wall. They could hear, in the hall, Grandprof counting louder and louder until he was shouting.

'Ninety-eight, ninety-nine, ONE HUNDRED! READY OR NOT HERE I COME,' and making a lot of noise as he stomped up the stairs.

Perdita stretched out her legs under the sofa and bounced Laura on her knee. Laura was the quietest of the little ones, which was useful. 'Why do we have to be in pairs?' she said. 'I mean, you're a very nice pair.'

Uncle Zac grinned and then looked serious. 'Actually, it's your Granny,' he said. 'She read a poem once about a game of hide and seek where somebody hid in an old trunk, and the lid came down on her and locked itself. And everybody looked for her and couldn't find her, so in the end they gave up.' He paused, as if to think about it, and Perdita, who had read a lot of stories in which bad things happened, had the distinct impression that he was about to change the ending. 'And she didn't get out until the next morning,' Uncle Zac said. 'So I think Granny's worried in case one of you gets stuck in a trunk.'

'Something like that,' said Grandprof, sticking his head over the back of the sofa. 'Boo!'

Of course the trouble with hide and seek is that if it takes a long time to find somebody – and in this case, Grandprof took a long time to find Uncle Mike and Max, who had hidden themselves in the airing cupboard on the landing, and had actually gone to sleep – then everyone else has to sit around waiting. So they changed the game to something that each family had a different name for: British Bulldog, or Kick the Can, or Twenty Twenty – but it was the same game. It was like hide and seek, but the idea was that while everyone started off by hiding, they really had to get back to where they started without 'It' catching them. Seeing that Tolpuddle Grange had back stairs, it was the ideal house for playing this game in.

Grandprof retired to his chair by the fire in the library and Uncle Mike prowled the corridors while people ran in all directions and hid in doorways. Perdita, thinking about it that evening, just remembered running and dodging and hiding until she was out of breath.

Then they played it again, with Daddy as 'It', and Perdita hid in her Mummy and Daddy's room behind their bed, and Daddy came racing through and caught Dulcie who was hiding in the bathroom, and they both ran out onto the landing and ran down the stairs. Perdita crept out from behind the bed, and through the bathroom, and onto her own bed, and drew the duvet up around her, and tried to look like a lump of bedclothes.

There was more running and cheerful shouting. Perdita lay quietly, privately rather glad of a break, wondering whether she had time to read a chapter of something.

When, above her head there was a creak and a thump, and she looked up. The cracks in the ceiling that had looked a bit like the map of Africa, suddenly started to snake outwards until it looked more like a hippopotamus, and there a cracking and splintering noise, and before Perdita had time to put her arm up to protect herself from whatever was happening, a slab of the ceiling buckled downwards and Dulcie slid down it and landed neatly, on her feet, on Sebastian's bed, along with a cloud of dust and bits of plaster and some very big spiders.

Perdita sat up and looked at her. Dulcie looked down at her feet, brushed vaguely at the front of her dress, and said, 'Hi, Perdy. I was in the attic,' and bounced off the bed and dashed out of the door.

Perdita watched her go, wondering quite what she should do. She got out of bed, and stepped on something hard. She bent down to see. It was the purse that had been in her skirt pocket and which she had completely forgotten about. She picked it up and put it under her pillow so that she wouldn't forget it again, and went downstairs.

Daddy came running out of the living room and pointed at her. 'Twenty twenty!' he shouted. 'You're in!'

'Dulcie's fallen through the ceiling,' Perdita said.

'You won't catch me like that,' Daddy said, and dashed into the library.

Dulcie appeared from under the stairs and dashed into the living room.

Daddy appeared, slid on the stone floor, and sprinted down the corridor and into the gun room.

Dulcie careened out of the living room and into the library.

Perdita walked down to the bottom of the stairs and walked very carefully into the library. Grandprof was sitting in one of the high-backed chairs, reading.

'Dulcie's fallen through the ceiling,' Perdita said.

Grandprof looked over the side of his chair. 'So that's why she's covered with dust,' he said, and went back to his book.

Daddy ran past the door, and Dulcie dodged out from behind Grandprof's chair and disappeared into the corridor.

Perdita gave up, and went and sat in the chair opposite Grandprof, and looked at the fire. It was very comforting.

And then Mummy came in and said, 'Perdy. What *have* you been doing? There's a great big hole in your bedroom ceiling!' and Perdita burst into tears.

Chapter 15

In Which there is a Headless Ghost, and a Stick-in-the-Mud

After that, things calmed down a little. Uncle Zac and Uncle Mike, both very practical men, set about mending the hole in the attic floor – or Perdita's ceiling – depending on how you looked at it. Mummy took Perdita into the kitchen and gave her a cup of sweet tea, which Granny said was good for shock. Daddy took everyone else out for a walk in the snow, and Jake took his rod and line and some sweetcorn and tried to catch another fish, but didn't. And they made some more snow cars and raced them until tea time. Perdita watched from the library window, and by the time they all came in, she was feeling like Perdita again.

~

It was Aunty Rill's turn to tell them a story after tea. She sat on the sofa in the library, and Daddy silently went and sat at the piano.

'OK, guys,' Aunty Rill said. 'Who's been to the Tower of London?'

Jake and Josie put their hands up.

'And who knows why it's called the Bloody Tower?'

'Because it's where people got their heads chopped off,' Jake said.

'Henry the Eighth,' Sebastian said.

'That's right,' Aunty Rill said cheerfully. 'And who was Anne Boleyn?'

'She was Henry the Eighth's second wife,' Sebastian said.

'And Queen Elizabeth's mummy,' Josie said. They all looked at her. 'Well, I know *some* things,' she said.

'Anyway,' Aunty Rill said, 'King Henry had poor Anne's head chopped off, and there's a legend, a legend, that her ghost walks around the Tower of London at night with her head underneath her arm.' Aunty Rill demonstrated with a cushion, and said, 'Take it, maestro' to Daddy, who played some rumbling low notes on the piano, and Aunty Rill began to sing…

'In the tower of London, large as life, the ghost of Anne Boleyn walks they declare.
Poor Anne Boleyn was once King Henry's wife until he made the headsman bob her hair.
Ah, yes, he did her wrong long years ago and she comes up at night to tell him so,

With her head tucked underneath her arm she walks the bloody tower,
With her head tucked underneath her arm at the midnight hour.

'She comes to haunt King Henry. She means giving him what for.
Gadzooks, she's going to tell him off for having spilt her gore

And just in case the headsman wants to give her an encore,
She has her head tucked underneath her arm.

'Come on … the chorus…

'*With her head tucked underneath her arm she walks the bloody tower,*
With her head tucked underneath her arm at the midnight hour.

'Along the draughty corridors for miles and mile she goes
She often catches cold, poor soul; it's cold there when it blows,
And it's awfully awkward for the queen to have to blow her nose
With her head tucked underneath her arm…

'*With her head tucked underneath her arm she walks the bloody tower,*
With her head tucked underneath her arm at the midnight hour.'

~

On her way up to her bath, Perdita overheard some discussion between Granny and Daddy about whether that had been a good song to sing and whether it might give Dulcie nightmares. Daddy said that he didn't think anything would give Dulcie nightmares, and Grandprof, who was coming downstairs, said that it had given him nightmares, but that was seventy years ago, and Dulcie was made of tougher stuff. Perdita got into her bath thinking that it wasn't Dulcie they had to worry about. There were plenty of empty corridors that people without heads might walk down, quite nearby, and so it was a relief to have an Uncle Charlie story before they went to bed.

They were sitting around the fire in the living room. Daddy had been playing Christmas carols, and when they all had had their baths, and Aunty Rill had brought in a tray of her special hot chocolate, Daddy came over and sat on the sofa.

'How about an Uncle Charlie story?' he said. 'I think we've had enough legends for one day.'

For one or two seconds, Perdita thought: but Jake and Josie and Uncle Mike are here and Uncle Charlie doesn't *belong* to them, but almost in the same second, she thought that Uncle Charlie would be a good Christmas present that she could share.

Daddy had obviously read her mind.

He said, 'Now, Jake and Josie – this is a story – a TRUE story – about my Grandfather and his brother Charlie – and they used to get into all sorts of trouble. At least Charlie did. And he was very unlucky. I mean, he was the sort of person who if there was something to fall into he would fall into it. And I got to thinking of him when I saw the sluice up by the ponds.

'You see, my Grandfather and Great-Uncle Charlie and the village boys had to walk to school every morning, and they had to go past a big pond that fed the canal. You know that when canals go up over hills, they have to be kept full of water when people let the water out to go down through the locks…' He looked at his audience. Sebastian and Jake were nodding sagely, and Josie and Dulcie were looking mystified. 'Well, that doesn't matter,' Daddy said, hastily. 'What matters is that there was a canal, and next to it were some ponds – just like the ones out there – and my Grandad and Uncle Charlie and their mates were walking past them on the way to school.

'So, one morning, on the way to school, they were playing pirates, and they had two gangs – two crews. Grandfather was one pirate chief, and Uncle Charlie was the other pirate chief, and they had a big fight, and Grandfather's gang captured Uncle Charlie's gang, and they decided to make Charlie walk the plank.'

'A real plank?' said Jake,

'As real as ever was,' said Daddy. 'They got a plank from somewhere, and stuck it out over the pond and made Charlie walk down it. When he got to the end, he wasn't all that keen to step off, but they joggled plank until he fell off.'

'Into the pond?' said Dulcie.

'Yup. Splash.'

'Didn't he drown?' said Perdita, even though she knew he couldn't have.

'No,' said Daddy. 'And you know why he didn't drown? Because the pond was only about half a metre deep. The water only came up to Charlie's knees.'

'So that was OK,' Josie said.

'Well, no,' Daddy said. 'The trouble was that Charlie went in feet first and his boots got stuck in the mud at the bottom of the pond and he couldn't move. So Great-Grandfather and the rest of them threw things at him for a bit, mud and stuff, and then they went off to school and left him standing in the pond.'

'All day?' said Jake.

'Well it would have been at least until lunchtime because that was the soonest that they could have got out of school. So there was Charlie standing there with his boots full of water and stuck in the mud.

Jake was thinking about this. 'Couldn't he just step out of his boots? Take them off, and wade out?'

'Well, no,' Daddy said, again. 'Have you tried to get your wellies off without bending down or touching them, or putting one heel on the other heel to get the other off? So he just had to stand there, and the occasional duck would come by and quack at him.

'But after about an hour, a narrowboat came by on the canal, and the narrowboat people saw him, and stopped, and they tied up the narrowboat and tried to get him out of the pond. First of all they tried to reach him with an oar, but he was too far from the side. Then the man on the narrowboat took off his boots and rolled up his trousers and stepped into the pond, but the mud was so soft on the bottom that he sank in too, and only just managed to haul himself out, and he was soaking as well. So they thought about it, and they thought that the only way to get Charlie out was to open the sluice and let the water out of the pond and into the canal. Then the water would go down, and then they could see if they could get Charlie out.

'Well, it worked. They wound the sluice gate up and the water ran out into the canal. And after about an hour the water level had dropped so far that you could see the tops of Charlie's boots, and after another half hour it was almost empty, and there was nothing but a lot of smelly mud, with dead fish and rotten weed, and all sorts of old rubbish, and Uncle Charlie standing there in his boots.

'So then the narrowboat people got two long planks – because narrowboats carry all sorts of things – put them down on the mud, and they crawled along to Charlie and pulled him out of his boots, and left the boots just sticking up there, empty. Then they put him onto the narrowboat, and rubbed him down and lent him some new boots and gave him something to eat and some hot tea – because he was really frozen. Then they put the planks back on the boat and closed the sluice, and the pond began to fill up again.'

'What about his boots?' said Sebastian.

'They just left them there, standing empty and sticking up out of the water,' Daddy said. 'So there was Charlie, chugging down the canal with the narrowboat people, and naturally, they asked him how he came to be stuck in the mud. So he told them that he was a poor orphan whose mummy and daddy had perished in a railway accident, and he had been living with his wicked aunt and uncle who starved him and beat him and made him work for nothing, and when he had tried to run away, they had thrown him in the pond to try to drown him, and they had left him to starve and die there sticking in the mud.

'And he was so convincing that the narrowboat people were very sorry for him, and took him to the next town, and left him at the police station.

'Meanwhile, back at the ponds, when it got to lunchtime, Grandfather sneaked out of school and ran back to see what had happened to Charlie. And what did he see? Just a pair of empty boots sticking out of the water! So, what could he do? He ran back home to his Mummy – that's Great-Great Granny, and told her all about it. And as you can imagine she was VERY cross, and she said she'd Deal With Him Later. Then she put her hat on and went to the Police Station to report Charlie missing!

'And when she said that a boy had run away and had fallen into the ponds, the policemen arrested her for being a cruel and wicked Aunt, and actually put her in a jail cell! And it was only when Great-Great Grandfather came home and found out what had happened and went down to the Police Station to explain, that they let her out.

'And I won't tell you what happened to my Grandfather and Uncle Charlie then, because I'm not allowed to tell you horrible stories.'

~

When Daddy came to put their lights out, Perdita and Sebastian were standing by the window, looking out at the snowy lawn. The moon had come out, and everything looked most odd: the light from the snow seemed to throw shadows upwards, so that the dark trees on each side of the lawn seemed darker, but Perdita said: 'There's something wrong with the clouds.'

Daddy came and looked. 'Do you know, I think its going to rain.'

'But it can't. What about the snow?' said Sebastian.

'That,' Daddy said, 'is a very good question.'

27 DECEMBER

Chapter 16

In Which it Rains. Rather a Lot Lot

Perdita woke up to rain. It was very noisy rain, and the light in the room was somehow different.

Sebastian was reading.

'It's raining,' he said, as she went past him to look out of the window. There was no sign of Dulcie.

Perdita looked out. She had read lots of times about people looking at things with dismay, but this was the first time she'd found herself doing it. It was raining hard, which was not a bad thing in itself, as she rather liked rain, but the snow … The snow had almost gone from the lawns: there were lumps where they had made the snow cars, and as she watched, Jake, wearing his pyjamas and a raincoat and wellies ran down the steps from the veranda and across to the remains of the snowman, now little more than a heap, and pushed it down the ha-ha, and then ran back inside. The rain swept along the veranda and slapped against the window.

'Well,' Mummy said, 'that is a bit of a pain.' She had come into Perdita's room in her dressing gown and was looking over Perdita's head at the rainy day. 'And we had such plans for today. Last day. We thought we might go to the seaside, and we had a nice surprise for you, too.

But I don't think any of that's going to happen. We'll have to have a family conference.'

So, by the time they had all got dressed and came down to the kitchen, Perdita was expecting to find gloom and doom. In fact, the kitchen was full of laughing. Daddy and Aunty Rill were having a pancake competition. Dulcie and Josie had been mixing the batter, and Granny had been looking at the AGA in a worried sort of way.

Daddy said: 'OK, what shall we put in our pancakes?'

'Raspberry jam with bacon bits in it,' Perdita said immediately.

'I liked it when you did fried cornflakes,' Dulcie said.

'You three,' said Mummy. 'They're always experimenting with horrible food,' she said to the world in general.

'I read that there's more protein in mouse than anything,' Uncle Zac said. He was sitting in the corner bouncing Laura on his knee. Uncle Zac was a good baby bouncer.

'And think yourself lucky you don't live in some countries,' Daddy said. 'Look at your Uncle Andrew when he was in Arabia somewhere. He went out to dinner with some great Sheikh in a tent in the desert, and they had a whole roast goat.'

'What's wrong with that?' Aunty Cass said. 'Sounds OK.' She was working her way through the cupboards to see how much food they had left.

'Nothing,' Daddy said. 'Except that because he was the honoured guest he got the best bit.' There was a pause. 'Aren't you going to ask?' Daddy said.

'Nobody dares,' Mummy said.

'They brought the goat's head, and presented it to him, and then they got a huge knife and chopped the head open, and scooped out the brains and gave them to him. Big treat. What's the matter, Dulcie?'

'Can we have the pancakes without eggshell this time?' Mummy said. 'I know there's lots of calcium and stuff, but it's too crunchy.'

'Fuss pot,' Aunty Rill said. 'You should live where they eat locusts. Snakes. Things like that. What shape pancake would you like, Dulcie?'

'A giraffe,' Dulcie said.

'How about a pig?' Aunty Rill said, looking into her frying pan. 'It looks like a pig.'

'It looks like a fish,' Dulcie said.

'What's the worst thing you ever ate?' Sebastian said, to the kitchen at large.

'Andouille,' said Aunty Rill without hesitation. 'It's a French sausage made of the inside of pigs. Smells like a pig-sty.'

'Oh, I liked that,' Grandprof said, coming into the kitchen holding a book. 'It looks great: nice fat pale sausage. Until you slice it. Then it smells like Uncle Charlie did when he fell in the pig trough.'

'Not over breakfast, please,' Granny said.

Perdita said, 'Daddy. You're burning that pancake!' and Daddy, who had been listening and forgotten for a moment that he was holding the pan, said, 'Right, stand back,' and tossed the pancake. Half of it landed back in the pan, and the other half was cut off neatly and landed on the floor. Aunty Cass picked up Max and sat him on her lap before he could get to it. 'Sorry Perdy ,' Daddy said. 'There's quite a lot left. I'll make another.'

By the time he had put more batter into his pan, Dulcie was eating her pig, with sugar and lemon, and Aunty Rill had cooked the next pancake. 'Who wants one that looks like Australia?'

'The worst thing I ever ate,' Daddy went on, 'was actually fish. In the north of Sweden, they have a kind of herring. They chop their heads off, and drop them into barrels of salt-water.'

'Then what?' Perdita said.

'Then nothing,' Daddy said. 'They leave them for six months.'

'Don't they go bad?' Sebastian said.

'You bet,' Daddy said. He tossed his pancake and it landed neatly in the pan. Aunty Rill tossed hers even higher, and caught it on a plate.

'Stop it you two,' Granny said. 'Somebody's got to wash the floor.'

'They go very bad,' Daddy said, sliding the pancake onto Perdita's plate. She looked at it. 'It's an armadillo,' Daddy said. 'So, these Swedish fish. They put them in tins. Then they leave them for a couple of years. Then they ferment in the tin, like the apple juice Josie left in her lunch box all last holiday.'

'But that was foul,' Aunty Cass said. 'Absolutely foul. Especially getting it off the ceiling.'

'It is,' Daddy said. 'The fish gives off gas, and the tins get rounder and rounder, and people keep them in their cellars – one year old and the tin is a bit round, two years old, it's a lot rounder. I went to dinner once and they gave us some of this. They got this round tin out, and then they stabbed it with a sharp tin-opener, and this, this smell shot out all over the kitchen, then they opened the tin and put this fish on the plate. And it just lay there, bubbling and luminous with rot.'

'It means you can see it in the dark,' Sebastian said.

'And I thought the Swedes were nice people,' Aunty Cass said.

'Aw, that's tame stuff,' said Uncle Zac. 'When Aunty Fee and I lived in China we had things like roast chicken's head, chickens' feet with jelly – you suck the claws and then crunch them up. Duck stomach. Pig brain.'

'OK,' Uncle Mike said. He had been calmly eating toast and marmalade, which, as he said, you didn't have to throw around. 'Who's coming log splitting.?'

~

After a lot of logs had been split, and the Uncles were barrowing them around to the front door, and it was still raining hard, it had been decided that driving to a wet beach would not be fun. Then Aunty Cass and Mummy had decreed that they were going to dry only one set of wet clothes for everybody, so they could choose how and when they wanted to get wet. Sebastian and Jake and Dulcie decided that they wanted to get wet fishing and Perdita and Josie decided that they didn't want to get wet at all, and spent a happy half hour playing Jenga in the playroom.

Then the soaked fishermen had come back in, deciding that sitting in a boat that was slowly filling up with water, watching their floats being knocked around by the rain hammering on the pond was no fun, and after they had been dried off, they all went and sat by the

Library fire, where Mummy was reading a story. One that was very wet.

'One day late in the autumn my master had a long journey to go on business. I was put into the dog-cart, and John went with his master. I always liked to go in the dog-cart, it was so light and the high wheels ran along so pleasantly. There had been a great deal of rain, and now the wind was very high and blew the dry leaves across the road in a shower. We went along merrily till we came to the toll-bar and the low wooden bridge. The river banks were rather high, and the bridge, instead of rising, went across just level, so that in the middle, if the river was full, the water would be nearly up to the woodwork and planks; but as there were good substantial rails on each side, people did not mind it.

'The man at the gate said the river was rising fast, and he feared it would be a bad night. Many of the meadows were under water, and in one low part of the road the water was halfway up to my knees; the bottom was good, and master drove gently, so it was no matter.

'When we got to the town of course I had a good bait, but as the master's business engaged him a long time we did not start for home till rather late in the afternoon. The wind was then much higher, and I heard the master say to John that he had never been out in such a storm; and so I thought, as we went along the skirts of a wood, where the great branches were swaying about like twigs, and the rushing sound was terrible.

"'I wish we were well out of this wood," said my master.

"'Yes, sir," said John, "it would be rather awkward if one of these branches came down upon us."

'The words were scarcely out of his mouth when there was a groan, and a crack, and a splitting sound, and tearing, crashing down among the other trees came an oak, torn up by the roots, and it fell right across the road just before us. I will never say I was not frightened, for I was. I stopped still, and I believe I trembled; of course I did not turn round or run away; I was not brought up to that. John jumped out and was in a moment at my head.

"'That was a very near touch," said my master. "What's to be done now?"

"'Well, sir, we can't drive over that tree, nor yet get round it; there will be nothing for it, but to go back to the four crossways, and that will be a good six miles before we get round to the wooden bridge again; it will make us late, but the horse is fresh."

'So back we went and round by the crossroads, but by the time we got to the bridge it was very nearly dark; we could just see that the water was over the middle of it; but as that happened sometimes when the floods were out, master did not stop. We were going along at a good pace, but the moment my feet touched the first part of the bridge I felt sure there was something wrong. I dare not go forward, and I made a dead stop. "Go on, Beauty," said my master, and he gave me a touch with the whip, but I dare not stir; he gave me a sharp cut; I jumped, but I dare not go forward.

"'There's something wrong, sir," said John, and he sprang out of the dog-cart and came to my head and looked all about. He tried to lead me forward. "Come on, Beauty, what's the matter?" Of course I could not tell him, but I knew very well that the bridge was not safe.

'Just then the man at the toll-gate on the other side ran out of the house, tossing a torch about like one mad.

"'Hoy, hoy, hoy! halloo! stop!" he cried.

"'What's the matter?" shouted my master.

"'The bridge is broken in the middle, and part of it is carried away; if you come on you'll be into the river."

"'Thank God!" said my master. "You Beauty!" said John, and took the bridle and gently turned me round to the right-hand road by the river side. The sun had set some time; the wind seemed to have lulled off after that furious blast which tore up the tree. It grew darker and darker, stiller and stiller. I trotted quietly along, the wheels hardly making a sound on the soft road. For a good while neither master nor John spoke, and then master began in a serious voice. I could not understand much of what they said, but I found they thought, if I had gone on as the master wanted me, most likely the bridge would have given way under us, and horse, chaise, master, and man would have fallen into the river; and as the current was flowing very strongly, and there was no light and no help at hand, it was more than likely we should all have been drowned. Master said, God had given men reason, by which they could find out things for themselves;

but he had given animals knowledge which did not depend on reason, and which was much more prompt and perfect in its way, and by which they had often saved the lives of men. John had many stories to tell of dogs and horses, and the wonderful things they had done; he thought people did not value their animals half enough nor make friends of them as they ought to do. I am sure he makes friends of them if ever a man did.

At last we came to the park gates and found the gardener looking out for us. He said that mistress had been in a dreadful way ever since dark, fearing some accident had happened, and that she had sent James off on Justice, the roan cob, toward the wooden bridge to make inquiry after us.

We saw a light at the hall-door and at the upper windows, and as we came up mistress ran out, saying, "Are you really safe, my dear? Oh! I have been so anxious, fancying all sorts of things. Have you had no accident?"

"'No, my dear; but if your Black Beauty had not been wiser than we were we should all have been carried down the river at the wooden bridge." I heard no more, as they went into the house, and John took me to the stable. Oh, what a good supper he gave me that night, a good bran mash and some crushed beans with my oats, and such a thick bed of straw! and I was glad of it, for I was tired.'

After that Granny and Mummy and Aunty Cass became very Firm and Efficient, and made everyone start to pack, because If They Didn't Do It Now they would Never Be Ready to Leave First Thing in the Morning.

Perdita felt rather sad about packing, because they seemed only just to have arrived, but she put the clothes she was going to wear the next day in the wardrobe, which was quite easy, as she was mostly going to wear the same ones as she was wearing today. Then she gathered up her books and spent half an hour searching the Library and the Playroom for any that had strayed. And it was only when she was straightening her bed that she trod on the little purse with the hard knobbly things in it that she had found hidden up the chimney. She pulled the string that was closing it, and tipped onto her bed – a bunch of keys.

Chapter 17

In Which there is a Lot of Searching. And Rain

Which was how they came to spend the afternoon trying every key in every keyhole in the whole huge house.

After some debate, which had been organised by Uncle Mike, who was good at this sort of thing, it was agreed that for every room, one person would hold the bunch of keys and the others would look for keyholes. So in the dining room, Perdita held the keys and Jake and Josie and Sebastian and Dulcie ran around looking for keyholes. There were quite a few in the cabinets around the walls, but the keys, when Perdita tried them, were too big and the wrong shape. This was very disappointing, so they went next door to the living room and Jake took the keys.

They hunted a long time, and all they could find was the keyhole to the door into the room (too big), the keyhole for the piano lid (too small), and the keyhole for the French Windows (which already had a key in it). There were no keyholes on the bookcases, but Dulcie found one on each of the little square fireside stools. One of the keys very nearly fitted – Jake could push it in, but not turn it: but you could open the lids anyway and there was nothing inside.

They'd moved on to the playroom, where Aunty Fee and Laura and Amelia were sitting by the fire, and Josie was trying the keyholes in all the trunks and the keys were almost the right size – they certainly looked the right age – when Grandprof came and stood in the doorway.

'I've just had the Colonel on the phone, and he said, he didn't know about the keys, but he thinks it's very exciting, and he hopes you'll find something. But not to get your hopes up, because he thinks that he and his sisters would have found any locked drawers, and they had a big clear out when the family moved out – lots of old trunks. But keep going, you never know. '

'That wasn't what he rang for?' said Uncle Mike.

'No,' Grandprof said. 'He said would we mind checking that the drains round the side of the house weren't clogged because sometimes there was a bit of a flood, and that could get into the cellar. And,' Grandprof paused, 'he said he forgot to tell us not to try using the metal door in the dining room fireplace if there was a wind, and especially a westerly, like yesterday. Because the smoke goes everywhere,'

'Always useful to know these things,' Uncle Mike said, and went across the hall to put his waterproofs on.

Daddy took over the supervision of the key quest, but they couldn't seem to find the right keyhole for any of the keys. The cupboards in the library and the gunroom seemed particularly promising, but none of the cupboards were locked. The same was true of the utility room and the Butler's Pantry. They were shooed out of the kitchen by Mummy and Granny, who had emptied all the food cupboards and were calculating what they had left to eat, and whether there would be enough milk for breakfast. All the cupboards were quite new and didn't have locks anyway, which Aunty Cass said was a pity with Max about. In the bedrooms the chests of drawers all had keyholes, and the wardrobes, and the drawers under the wardrobes had more – but never of a size or shape anything like the keys on the bunch.

When they got to the attic, where they could hear the rain drumming on the roof tiles, there was a pause while Uncle Zac, who had been tinkering with the model railway, shone his torch under all the eaves, but there was only the dressing-up box, and that didn't have a keyhole, and some tea chests that didn't have lids. By this time, Dulcie and Josie had rather lost interest, and stayed with Uncle Zac, as he fiddled with batteries and wires, but Perdita and Jake kept going.

Halfway down the back stairs was a tall wall-cupboard, and to their delight (another thing Perdita had not thought very likely to happen in real life) one key fitted and clicked in the lock, and the door opened. She and Jake and Daddy almost bumped heads looking in. But the cupboard was bare.

'At least they're real keys,' Jake said, meaning, Perdita thought, that they belonged to the house.

But that was all the luck they had. The fuse box for all the electrics had a door with a keyhole, but it was half open. The big wooden box in the playroom which held the table-tennis bats and old nets had a keyhole, but the lid was open and no keys fitted anyway. The last hope was the cellar. The low door at the end of the playroom had a keyhole, but it was a modern one, and the door wasn't locked. Daddy pushed it open and felt for the light switch. The single bulb showed the huge white boiler, simmering away, and the arched vaults with their boxes of shrivelled apples, and sacks of coal. But as much as Daddy swept the torch into the corners they could see nothing that a key would fit.

They came back to the kitchen, rather dispirited, to find a Great Frying going on. Perdita put the keys down on the work surface by the door.

'We're having bubble-and-squeak made of everything we can find for tea,' Aunty Rill said. 'There's going to be just enough – although for some reason there are three litres of vegetable oil and six huge packets of crisps left. There's eggs and bread for breakfast, and just enough milk for grown-up tea tomorrow morning, so no milk for cornflakes. Except there aren't any cornflakes left anyway.'

'And those chocolate biscuits are a treat for the journey home,' Granny said. 'I've counted them.' Perdita looked at her carefully to see whether she was joking, but it was very difficult to tell.

~

They were finishing the bubble-and-squeak, and seeing who could squeeze the last squirt of tomato ketchup out of the bottle, when Daddy stood up and tapped on the edge of the nearest frying pan. (Granny and Aunty Rill had served the bubble-and-squeak straight out of the frying pans, which Perdita thought was Absolutely the Right Thing.)

'OK, listen up, troops,' he said. 'Very sad we're leaving in the morning after breakfast, so this evening we want to get the place tidied up and all ready to go, so after bath there's going to be a very quick story from Grandprof, and then we're all going to bed early. That is, you lot are going to bed early, and then a bit later, the grown-ups are going to bed early as well. So, go and play for an hour and then it's bath time. And don't fall though any ceilings or get stuck up any chimneys.'

Chapter 18

In Which there are Ghosts of One Kind and Another

Grandprof started his story a little later than he was meant to because just as he was going to, Uncle Mike and Jake and Sebastian came down to say that they'd got the train in the attic to work – or at least, Jake had – and the coloured-light signals, and the light on the front of the engine. And so everyone had to go up to see it working, including the Mummies. Perdita thought that it was one of the best things: with the lights out, and the rain raining, and the little headlight moving along the tracks. On the way down the stairs, she saw Jake take Sebastian to one side and whisper to him, but by the time she had caught up they had carried on down, both looking elaborately innocent.

When she got to the library, Grandprof was sitting on the sofa with some old books beside him, and Dulcie on his knee. Perdita sat down and leaned against his legs and looked into the fire, which was always interesting.

Grandprof looked at Jake and Sebastian. 'Some people have been nagging me all day to tell them a spooky story, so I've remembered one that is just a *little bit* spooky. Are you ready for a little bit spooky one?'

'If you must,' Mummy said.

'Well, it's more strange than spooky,' Grandprof said. 'It's about a ghost village, just along the coast.'

'Do you mean a village where there are ghosts?' Sebastian said.

'No,' Grandprof said. 'The whole village is a ghost. Have you heard stories of villages that have been flooded to make reservoirs, and people now can hear the church bells ringing, even if they're under water? The bells, that is. Well, this is about a village not far from here, called Tyneham.

'Once upon a time it was a small, peaceful village surrounded by gently sloping country, and you could walk down to the coast in about an hour if you wanted to. The name means "goat enclosure" if you were wondering, and it had a thirteenth-century church., and very old Elizabethan grange – a bit like this one, except older. It was such a quiet place that the school had to close because there weren't enough pupils.

'Well, just before Christmas in 1943, in the middle of the Second World War, the postman arrived with a letter for every household, telling them that the government needed somewhere to train soldiers and to practice shooting and blowing up things, so they had decided to take over thousands of acres of land. And, by bad luck, their village, Tyneham, was right in the middle of it, and so they had to leave – and leave within a month! Just before Christmas, too.

'Of course they didn't want to, but the government said it was vital for the war effort, and the army had to practise blowing things up somewhere, but that the villagers could come back after the war was over, if the army hadn't blown all their houses up. So everybody packed their things and left on the seventeenth of December. Two hundred and twenty-five people had to leave. One lady even left a message pinned to the Church door which said' (Grandprof looked at a book):

> '"Please treat the church and houses with care; we have given up our homes where many of us lived for generations to help win the war to keep men free. We shall return one day and thank you for treating the village kindly."

'But they never did come back. During the war, the army blew up some of the houses, and after the war, the government and the army broke their promise and bought all the land so they could practise shooting for ever. And the cottage roofs fell in, and the old grange became so dilapidated that it had to be pulled down. Isn't that sad?'

'Yes,' Perdita said. 'I think that's sad.' She looked at Sebastian and Jake, who clearly weren't thinking of it being sad, but were thinking about blowing things up.

'But,' Grandprof said, 'you can go there now and visit it, on days when the army isn't shooting things. You can go into the church, and the school – and you can see the school books still open on the desks. And you can walk along the streets, but most of the houses are just ruins.

'It's a very strange place, and most of the time it's very very quiet.' He lowered his voice. 'But there's one very strange and spooky thing. Right in the middle of the village, by the roadside in Post Office Row, is the old village phone box. It was the only phone in the village, because in those days they didn't have any mobile phones, and very very few people had their own phone in their own house.'

'They had one here,' Sebastian said. 'In the alcove in the hall.'

Grandprof nodded. 'But it seems in Tyneham there was one phone box for the whole village, and everyone shared it when they wanted to make a phone call.

'And, of course, when everybody left the village in 1943, it was disconnected. In those days all the phones were connected by land lines, strung from telephone poles for miles over the landscape. So, naturally, the army took the poles down and rolled up the wires. But the old phone box still stood there, with its phone in it, but it wasn't connected to anything.

'Now, a few years ago, some friends of mine went to visit the village – and it just happened to be on the seventeenth of December. It was a very cold and dingy and misty and foggy day, so there was hardly anyone about, and they walked around the village looking at the ruins of the old houses, and they came to Post Office Row, and there was the old phone box. And just as they came alongside the phone box – do you know what happened? The telephone in the telephone box rang by itself. My friends stopped and looked, and that old phone rang again and again. Eventually, one of my friends plucked up courage and opened the door and lifted the receiver. And he said, 'Hello?' and he heard someone breathing on the other end of the line, and then there was a click, and the phone went dead.

'Well, you can imagine they were pretty mystified about that, but then they found out that, over the years, and always on the seventeenth of December, the phone rings. Several people have heard it, and when they have had the nerve to pick up the phone – the line is always silent.'

'OK,' Mummy said. 'Thank you Grandprof. Up to bed, all of you. You can read for a bit, but we'll be up soon to put your lights out.'

~

Perdita lay in bed, looking at the ceiling, where Uncle Mike and Uncle Zac had patched it, in the light from the bathroom, and wondering why one had to 'pluck up' courage, when the door from the landing opened very quietly and slowly. It was Jake.

'Come on,' he said. 'Midnight feast!' He held out a carrier bag in one hand, and had a large black torch in his other.

The light from the landing seemed rather dim and cold, but it was enough for her to see Sebastian getting out of bed and putting his dressing gown and slippers on. She looked at her little glowing alarm clock. It was 9.15. Hardly midnight, but a lot later than she was usually awake. She got up and put on her dressing gown and slippers, and went out onto the landing, closing the door carefully behind her. Just as long as Dulcie didn't wake up – but she never did. Josie was there, in her dressing gown, looking a little wide-eyed and holding a very large teddy bear.

Jake tiptoed to the banister and put his finger to his lips. They listened: there were voices coming from the living room: the deep calm voice of Uncle Mike and the cheerful voice of Aunty Cass, and Mummy laughing. There were footsteps in the hall, and Perdita could just see Granny passing the foot of the stairs carrying a tray.

'Come on,' Jake whispered, and they went down the corridor past all the bedrooms, Jake leading, with Sebastian close behind, also carrying a torch, then Josie, still looking worried, and then Perdita, who was thinking that this may not be a good idea, but there wasn't much point in arguing with Jake. Still, it was quite fun to be creeping – another really good word – down corridors There was a nightlight in Laura and Amelia's room, and they tiptoed by, and then Jake and Sebastian switched on their torches, and they were going down the back stairs, and past the back door to the kitchen. It was slightly open, and Jake stopped, and they listened. It was absolutely quiet, and then they heard the baize door open and close. Jake switched off his torch, and Sebastian, after a slight fumble when Perdita thought he might drop it, switched his off too.

Somebody had come into the kitchen. There was the sound of a cupboard being opened, and a sliding noise, like a tin being moved, and then the noise of the kettle being switched on. Perdita knew that at a time like this you were supposed to desperately want to sneeze, and she found, not entirely to her surprise, that she actually *did* want to. She tried to breathe through her mouth only, and the kettle bubbled and clicked. Water was poured, and there was the sound of Daddy humming. He was humming the song that he always said he hated most: 'Jingle Bells'. Then the cupboard door was closed and soft footsteps went away across the kitchen and the baize door swung open and closed.

Jake's torch snapped on, and Josie sneezed into her teddy bear, and by torchlight they went quickly down the stairs into the games room. Jake threaded his way between the pool table and the table-tennis table and they arrived at the door into the cellar. Jake clicked the latch, and the door opened with a creaking sound. They stood still, but nothing happened. Jake felt around for the light switch and clicked it down. Nothing happened. He tried again. Still nothing.

Then he said, cheerfully, 'Never mind, better with torches,' and he pushed the door closed behind them. He swung his torch down, and there on the floor were four cushions. 'I smuggled them down earlier,' he said, sounding rather pleased with himself, and Perdita had to admit to that perhaps he had a right to be. Doing things that people did in books was always harder than you think. They sat down, each to a cushion. 'Isn't this great?' Jake said.

The boiler burbled behind them, which was a sort of comforting noise. Jake set his torch down so that the beam was pointing up at the curve of the ceiling; around them, the cellar was dark.

'They might be a bit cross if they find us,' Perdita said, cautiously. She couldn't quite make up her mind whether this was as exciting as midnight feasts were in books. Part of her was quite thrilled – another good word that made her feel as if something was happening to her spine – and part of her was Sensible Perdita.

'They won't,' Jake said, 'as long as we're not too very long.' He started to take things out of the carrier bag. There was a big bag of salt and vinegar crisps, and four chocolate biscuits, and a box of orange juice. 'Not a bad feast?' said Jake.

'But didn't Granny say she'd counted them?' Perdita said, pointing to the chocolate biscuits. 'She's bound to miss them.'

'Ah,' said Jake. 'I borrowed them *before* she counted them!' He tore the corner off the orange juice box. 'Same with this.'

And at that moment they heard the scratching. It came from somewhere in the corner of the cellar outside of the reach of the torchlight. They all froze, just as you were supposed to in books, with their biscuit or crisp or juice halfway to their mouths. Sebastian was the first to recover. He switched his torch on and shone it towards the sound. There was nothing but the arches of the cellar going back into the darkness.

They listened, but there was no more scratching, and they went on eating, rather nervously.

And then there was a hollow cooing noise.

'OK,' said Jake. 'Let's go,' but before he could move, they saw a pale light, and a white face lit from below appeared from the depths of the cellar. Josie dropped her biscuit with a squeak and clutched her teddy bear; Jake moved towards where the door must be, but knocked over the torch. Sebastian was trying to find his torch. But Perdita, after being frightened, found herself laughing. She swallowed and sang, '"With her head, tucked underneath her arm…" Hello, Aunty Rill.'

'Hi,' said Aunty Rill, directing her torch beam from underneath her chin to the bag of crisps. 'Tell you what. I won't tell anybody as long as you go straight back to bed and let me have a lot of crisps.'

~

Perdita had been in bed for no more than three minutes when Mummy put her head around the bathroom door to check that she was asleep. She kept her eyes closed and made 'I am asleep' noises. 'Sweet dreams,' Mummy said. 'See you in the morning,' and the bathroom door closed.

Perdita lay listening to the rain and thinking how nice it was to listen to the rain while you were going to sleep, and how nice it was to be going home tomorrow, and what a pity it was to be going home tomorrow. And what an odd thing to say, 'going to sleep' as if it were somewhere else that you went to, and perhaps it was, and she went to sleep, wherever it was.

28 DECEMBER

Chapter 19

In Which they are Completely Surrounded by Water

Aunty Rill was the first to leave. And the first to come back.

It had been a slightly sad morning, Perdita thought. There had been a lot of bags being packed and beds being stripped and the sheets and duvets folded on the ends of the beds, and luggage piled up in the hallway, and every now and then someone would dash out into the rain to one of the cars and jam something in, sometimes with somebody else holding an umbrella over them.

It had been raining all night, sometimes so hard that it woke Perdita, and she had got out of bed and put her head round the curtains and looked down at the garden. All the snow had gone, but in the grey light she could see wide pools of water lying across the grass. It wasn't like at home, where you could hear the rain on the roof: here it swept and swooshed across the windows and cascaded down splashing onto the terrace. Perdita had gone back to bed and was awoken by an argument going on in Mummy and Daddy's room, between Mummy and Sebastian and Dulcie who both wanted to go out and splosh in the puddles and Mummy said she sympathised but she wasn't going to have them soaking wet in the car going home, and why didn't they go and play with the trains in the attic as long as Dulcie promised not to fall through the ceiling again.

Perdita had washed and dressed, and packed her clothes, and put all her books in her book bag, and folded her bedclothes neatly. The room looked rather uncomfortable and deserted, so she went out into the corridor. All the doors were open, and Jake and Josie were carrying their bags down the stairs.

In the kitchen, Granny was cleaning the AGA, and there were two cardboard boxes on the table with what was left of the food (mostly packets of crisps, so it wasn't surprising that Granny hadn't missed one). Perdita had a sort of breakfast at one end of the table, consisting of a dippy egg and a glass of orange juice, and almost before she had finished, Grandprof, who was washing up anything that moved, as he said, had whisked her plate and spoon and egg cup and glass away to the sink.

Perdita was given the job of making sure that no books had been left behind, and found herself wandering through rooms that seemed to have got bigger as well as being just empty of life. The fires were just flattish heaps of ash, with the occasional charred piece of smouldering log. She found *A Christmas Carol*, of all things to forget, half-under a cushion in the library, and *Angelina's Christmas* under the sofa, and then she went back into the hall where something seemed to be happening.

What was mostly happening was Aunty Rill saying goodbye to everyone, which consisted of a lot of hugging and kissing and picking up and swinging around of the littlest ones. The fact that Aunty Rill was up at all slightly surprised Perdita, but as she had only a shoulder bag, and never seemed to carry anything with her, Perdita supposed that getting up and packing must be very easy.

It was still pouring with rain outside. Uncle Mike was packing bags into the back of the car with mathematical efficiency: he was, Perdita thought, the sort of man that the rain wouldn't really dare rain on. His waterproof was getting wet, of course, but you could see that the rain, heavy as it was, wasn't really trying to wet his head.

He waved to Aunty Rill as she ran across to her little sports car, and slid into the driver's seat, revved up the engine, and with a scrunch of gravel, she disappeared into the trees and down the drive.

Aunty Fee came out to start putting the babies in their car.

Granny and Grandprof came and gave them all a hug, and put their last case into the back of the big red Volvo, and Aunty Cass was trying to stop Josie hopping across to the car because she couldn't find her other boot, when there was a vroom noise and Aunty Rill's car came back into the drive and crunched to a halt. Everybody stopped what they were doing.

'OK. What have you forgotten?' Uncle Mike said.

'My amphibious pontoon,' Aunty Rill said, opening her car door. 'Without it I can't get out. The road's flooded.'

'How deep?' Grandprof said. Granny was sitting in the car, and he was leaning on his half-open car door.

'Don't know for sure,' Aunty Rill said. 'Far too deep for Angie, here. You can only just see the hedgetops on the Tolpuddle road.' She patted her car, and stood up, and loped across to the porch, and put her arm around Perdita, who happened to be nearest.

'We'll go and have a look,' Grandprof said. 'I've got the biggest wheels. Better get inside and wait.' He got into the Volvo and drove away. Aunty Fee carried Amelia, in her car seat, back into the house, and everyone else came and stood in the hall, not sure what to do. The rain rained harder.

About five minutes passed. Perdita sat in the porch on what was left of the log pile. Funny, it had been way higher than her head when they had arrived, and now it was only a few logs deep. She looked at them. They seemed very dry and spiders-webby. Perhaps they'd been there for years, and every year people just piled new ones on top. Perhaps a log pile was like rings on a tree, she thought. You could see how old a tree was by counting the rings, so you could tell how old a pile of logs was by counting …

She had got that far in the argument, when there was a crunching on the drive and Grandprof's Volvo came back. But it wasn't alone. Behind it was a green Land-Rover. A very familiar green Land-Rover. Perdita jumped up and ran to the door, and the Land-Rover stopped and her friends from the summer, Dancing Perdita, and Tim and Dan climbed out into the rain, and ran into the porch and Dulcie and Sebastian hugged them, and Mummy and Daddy hugged them, and Daddy introduced them to everyone else.

'But what are you doing here?' Perdita said, while Granny and Grandprof came damply back in, carrying their suitcases.

'This was yesterday's surprise,' Daddy said. 'These three just happened to be spending Christmas in Wareham, just down the road, so they said they'd come over yesterday, but what with all the weather, they're running a day late.'

'Emma's staying with her Aunty at Midsummer Farm,' Dan said, 'so you'll have to make do with the three of us.'

'And that may be longer than you think,' Grandprof said. He ran up three stairs and turned round and clapped his hands.

'Just so I can tell everyone at once,' he said. 'The River Piddle has been piddling a lot lot, with the snow and the rain, and Rill's right: there's no chance of getting across to Tolpuddle, so I thought we'd see how the road was if you go down the valley a bit, and cross over at Afpuddle, but halfway we met our friends coming the other way.'

Tim said, 'It was pretty bad all the way here from Wareham, but just past Afpuddle, the road dips and there's a flood there. We only just got through it, and there were two cars that tried to come through behind us, and the first one conked out.'

'It was awful, really,' Dancing Perdita said. 'The man had to get out and wade back and abandon his car. There wasn't anything we could do, and he just waved us to go on, and gave us the thumbs up. I think he must have been a local.'

'So now his car's blocking the road, even if we could get through again,' Dan said.

Aunty Cass, who was probably, Perdita thought, the most practical person in the room said, 'So are we stuck here or is there another way out? Can we get over the hills?'

Uncle Mike, probably the second most practical person, said, 'There are some tracks in the wood and farm tracks, but I wouldn't like to try it, even in a Land-Rover. They must be pretty bad, and you'd have to know where you're going.'

'I'll ring the Colonel,' Grandprof said. 'Looks like we're stuck for the rest of the day at least.'

'And it's still raining,' Mummy said.

Granny took charge. That was the sort of phrase Perdita had read a lot, but she had never seen it done, and it was pretty impressive. Granny moved Grandprof out of the way and stood on the stairs: 'Everyone take their wet things off! Zac, can you get the fires lighted again? And everyone else into the kitchen and we'll make some tea and get everyone dry. Mike, can you get the boxes of food out of the cars again, especially any milk if there's any left.' She went off to the kitchen. Behind her back, Daddy and the Uncles saluted and got to work.

The next quarter of an hour was spent taking off wet things, and bringing in suitcases and finding slippers and soon it was hardly possible to walk across the hall for open cases and bags. Then they had to show Dancing Perdita and Tim and Dan around the house.

When they got back to the kitchen, Grandprof was saying, 'He's put off the next bunch of people until at least tomorrow, and he doesn't think the roads will be passable until at least late this evening, if then. So he says, just stay another night.'

'That's all very well,' Granny said, 'but we can't all live on three packets of crisps.'

'There's four litres of vegetable oil,' Aunty Rill said, helpfully.

'And we've got all our Christmas chocolate,' Tim said. 'You must have, too.'

'Deep fried chocolate,' Granny said.

Uncle Mike said: 'There's the potato clamp. We could have chips as well as deep fried chocolate. And leeks and brassicas in the walled garden.'

'Well, that's something,' Granny said. She was lining their provisions up on the kitchen table. There were two bags of flour, four packets of crisps, two tins of Cannelloni beans, a packet of chocolate biscuits, two bananas, and some butter.

'There's lots of odds and ends like Worcester Sauce and mustard in the cupboards, that people obviously don't take home,' Mummy said.

'And there's some old apples in the cellar,' Sebastian said.

'And we all got pickles and cheese and biscuits and tins of pâté in our stockings,' Grandprof said. 'At least, I did.'

'I just wish we had some yeast so we could make bread,' Granny said.

'Loaves and fishes,' Sebastian said, and there was a knock on the back door. Perdita, who was nearest, opened it. Standing in the rain, with a big basket, was a boy. He was wearing a very wet waterproof, which looked as though it had stopped being waterproof some time ago, with a large hood.

'My grandmothers sent you some things,' he said. 'And I brought you a fish' and he held out the basket, which was covered with a tea towel. He lifted one edge of it, and there was a carp, the biggest fish that Perdita had ever seen.

~

'So that was George,' Mummy said, when things had been re-organised and Perdita and Granny and Mummy and Dancing Perdita were making bread, and Aunty Rill was expertly dealing with the carp. 'A guardian angel.' In the basket, apart from the fish, had been two bottles of milk, a bag of flour, and some yeast, which was now being put to good use.

George had come into the kitchen and shyly put the basket on the table, and then pushed his hood back. There was a very short silence, and Dulcie had said, 'Oh, your poor face. Did it hurt?' and he had smiled and said, 'It was a long time ago. I don't really remember,' and Jake said, 'Didn't I see you in the wood the other day?' and Sebastian said, 'Did you really catch that fish?' and in about three minutes George had stopped being shy, and everyone hardly noticed his scarred face any more, and it was arranged that there would be a fishing party so that George could show them how to catch more carp.

Uncle Mike and Sebastian and Jake and Dulcie and Dan took him into the gun room and he sorted out rods and lines and hooks – he had brought his own mysterious bait. And they put their wet weather gear on again, and Perdita had watched them from the window as George led them to the other side of the ponds from the sluice and they disappeared between the trees and the reed beds.

Uncle Zac came into the kitchen from lighting the three fires, in the living room, the library, and the playroom. They all were still smouldering from the night before, but it had taken some time to nurse them back to life without any kindling. But he had taken armfuls of logs from the porch, and the fires were now bright and burning.

'Just the man,' Granny said, as he went over to the AGA with the obvious intention of boiling the kettle. 'We need some potatoes and some leeks, Zac. We're making a big stew for lunch,' and Uncle Zac obediently went and put his boots and waterproof on, and went out into the rain.

When the bread was proving, and there didn't seem much for her to do, Perdita went to find Grandprof in the Library,

'Ah,' he said. 'They're making stew, I hear.' He had two books open on the sofa. Perdita settled down beside him.

'It was still early when we got settled, and George said that, as we had plenty of time, it would be a splendid opportunity to try a good, slap-up supper. He said he would show us what could be done up the river in the way of cooking, and suggested that, with the vegetables and the remains of the cold beef and general odds and ends, we should make an Irish stew.

'It seemed a fascinating idea. George gathered wood and made a fire, and Harris and I started to peel the potatoes. I should never have thought that peeling potatoes was such an undertaking. The job turned out to be the biggest thing of its kind that I had ever been in. We began cheerfully, one might almost say skittishly, but our light-heartedness was gone by the time the first potato was finished. The more we peeled, the more peel there seemed to be left on; by the time we had got all the peel off and all the eyes out, there was no potato left—at least none worth speaking of. George came and had a look at it—it was about the size of a peanut. He said:

"'Oh, that won't do! You're wasting them. You must scrape them."

'So we scraped them, and that was harder work than peeling. They are such an extraordinary shape, potatoes—all bumps and warts and hollows. We worked steadily for five-and-twenty minutes, and did four potatoes. Then we struck. We said we should require the rest of the evening for scraping ourselves.

'I never saw such a thing as potato-scraping for making a fellow in a mess. It seemed difficult to believe that the potato-scrapings in which Harris and I stood, half smothered, could have come off four potatoes. It shows you what can be done with economy and care.

'George said it was absurd to have only four potatoes in an Irish stew, so we washed half a dozen or so more, and put them in without peeling. We also put in a cabbage and about half a peck of peas. George stirred it all up, and then he said that there seemed to be a lot of room to spare, so we overhauled both the hampers, and picked out all the odds and ends and the remnants, and added them to the stew. There were half a pork pie and a bit of cold boiled bacon left, and we put them in. Then George found half a tin of potted salmon, and he emptied that into the pot.

'He said that was the advantage of Irish stew: you got rid of such a lot of things. I fished out a couple of eggs that had got cracked, and put those in. George said they would thicken the gravy.

'I forget the other ingredients, but I know nothing was wasted; and I remember that, towards the end, Montmorency (he's the dog), who had evinced great interest in the proceedings throughout, strolled away with an earnest and thoughtful air, reappearing, a few minutes afterwards, with a dead water-rat in his mouth, which he evidently wished to present as his contribution to the dinner; whether in a sarcastic spirit, or with a genuine desire to assist, I cannot say.

'We had a discussion as to whether the rat should go in or not. Harris said that he thought it would be all right, mixed up with the other things, and that every little helped; but George stood up for precedent. He said he had never heard of water-rats in Irish stew, and he would rather be on the safe side, and not try experiments.

'Harris said: "If you never try a new thing, how can you tell what it's like? It's men such as you that hamper the world's progress. Think of the man who first tried German sausage!"

'It was a great success, that Irish stew. I don't think I ever enjoyed a meal more. There was something so fresh and piquant about it. One's palate gets so tired of the old hackneyed things: here was a dish with a new flavour, with a taste like nothing else on earth.

'And it was nourishing, too. As George said, there was good stuff in it. The peas and potatoes might have been a bit softer, but we all had good teeth, so that did not matter much: and as for the gravy, it was a poem—a little too rich, perhaps, for a weak stomach, but nutritious.'

'Mmm,' said Perdita.

'OK,' said Grandprof, 'how about …

'The gipsy grumbled frightfully, and declared if he did a few more deals of that sort he'd be ruined. But in the end he lugged a dirty canvas bag out of the depths of his trouser pocket, and counted out six shillings and sixpence into Toad's paw. Then he disappeared into the caravan for an instant, and returned with a large iron plate and a knife, fork, and spoon. He tilted up the pot, and a glorious stream of hot, rich stew gurgled into the plate. It was, indeed, the most beautiful stew in the world, being made of partridges, and pheasants, and chickens, and hares, and rabbits, and peahens, and guinea-fowls, and one or two other things. Toad took the plate on his lap, almost crying, and stuffed, and stuffed, and stuffed, and kept asking for more, and the gipsy never grudged it him. He thought that he had never eaten so good a breakfast in all his life.'

'That's better,' Perdita said, and they sat reading companionably by the fire, and Perdita was vaguely aware of people moving around the house, and doors opening and closing, and Uncle Zac coming in with more logs.

'Did you know,' Grandprof said. 'That this is the third day of Christmas?'

'Of course,' said Perdita. 'On the third day of Christmas my true love gave to me,

> Three French hens,
> Two calling birds,
> And a partridge in a Pear tree.'

'I've found,' Grandprof said, 'an old French version: it translates as

> "One boneless stuffing,
> Two breasts of veal,
> Three joints of beef,
> Four pig's trotters,
> Five legs of mutton,
> Six partridges with cabbage,
> Seven spitted rabbits,
> Eight plates of salad,
> Nine dishes for a chapterful of canons,
> Ten full casks,
> Eleven pretty maidens,
> And twelve Musketeers."'

'I think I prefer a partridge in a pear tree,' Perdita said. And then it was lunchtime.

They went into the kitchen, which was warm and steamy again, and smelt of all sorts of things, and Aunty

Rill was describing how one pan was leek and potato soup or stew, and the other was everything else they could find stew, and there was no doubt that it all smelt most sentimental.

'And it's fish and chips for supper,' Aunty Rill said, waving at a vast serving dish on the work surface next to the AGA, where there were five huge carp, their scales shining silver and with a pale gold sheen. Perdita felt rather sorry for them, and then at the same time thought they were very ugly, too, with humped backs and strange round scales, and it looked as though they had four eyes.

'Did you catch all those?' she said.

''I caught the biggest one, the one on the top,' Jake said. 'And Josie caught that one.' He poked a fish.

'It was humiliating,' Uncle Mike said, cheerfully. 'There was a path through the reeds, and he simply stopped every now and then, and showed us where to cast and in two minutes we had these carp. We've been trying for three days.'

'And he didn't need to use a spod,' Jake said.

They sat around the table, and Aunty Rill went around with two mugs of soup and a teaspoon and everyone tried a taste of both soups.

'And when you've finished lunch,' Daddy said, 'everyone can do what they like for an hour – inside…' He glanced at the window, where the rain was still sloshing down. 'But, whatever you do, you Must Not Go Into the Living Room.'

'Why not?' said Sebastian.

'Because you'll be turned into a goonie!' said Mummy, who then obviously wished she hadn't because everyone started singing 'Little Bunny Foo Foo' until Granny said that if they didn't stop she'd tell them what was in the stews, and so they stopped and ate the stews and the bread, until they were all gone.

Chapter 20

*In Which there is an Unexpected Show, and
an Even More Unexpected Diary*

After lunch, Perdita went back to the study again, and read *The Wind in the Willows* for what seemed like a few minutes, until Mummy put her head around the door.

'Ah, there you are. Could you round everybody up? Tell them there's a palaver, and an *indaba*, and a *punchayet*, and a *pow-wow* in the living room in ten minutes, and that includes Sebastian and Jake.'

Perdita stopped to count, and decided that there must be nineteen people to round up, not counting herself. She went through the kitchen where Granny and Mummy were peeling potatoes, and down to the playroom. Uncle Mike and Aunty Rill and Tim the Archaeologist and Daddy were playing running round the table table-tennis. She delivered her message, and went up the back stairs to the attic, which was fairly crowded with railway enthusiasts. She had to shout a bit to get their attention, but after a while the buzzing of the trains stopped. And people started to come downstairs.

At the first landing, she turned into the bedroom corridor and immediately found Dulcie and Josie, who had got their dolls out of the cars and were playing hospitals in the first bedroom. Perdita shooed them downstairs and followed them down to tha hall.

Aunty Fee was coming downstairs with the baby, and she could see that there was nobody in the library or the playroom, so went into living and stopped dead.

In the middle of the room, being admired by Daddy and Uncle Zac, and being adjusted by Dancing Perdita and Dan, was a Punch and Judy show: a tall, stripy box with a proscenium arch on the top, and Dancing Perdita and Dan were dressed in stripy clothes, too.

'It's our new thing,' Dancing Perdita said. And they all gathered into the room. Uncle Zac put some more logs on the fire. 'Dan is training to be a Professor – all the people who run Punch and Judy shows are called Professor. Have you ever seen a Punch and Judy Show?'

Perdita hadn't, and for the next half hour it was like living in a mad world where anybody who wasn't laughing was going 'Oh, no!' or, in the case of Laura, hiding her head in her father's sweater, or, in the case of Jake, jumping up and down and running around the room and sitting down again in excitement.

First, Professor Dan showed them a strange little metal thing called a swazzle – and then he put it into his mouth and his voice changed into a rasping, whistly one, and the show began.

Dan disappeared behind the curtain, and Mr Punch appeared with his little black and white dog, Toby, and then they danced with Judy, who had a baby with her. They did a wild dance and then Judy (whose voice was rather like Dancing Perdita's) asked him to look after the baby while she went shopping. So first of all Mr Punch kept throwing the baby out into the audience and they kept picking it up and giving it back to him. After the third time, Mr Punch decided to put the baby into a sausage machine (much shrieking from the audience, including, Perdita realised, with a bit of a shock, herself). Then Judy came back and wanted to know where the baby was, and Punch tried to get rid of her by hitting her with a big stick. Whereupon Judy got a bigger stick and hit him back,

Then a policeman came in to arrest Mr Punch and hit him with his truncheon, whereupon Mr Punch hit the policeman with his stick, and the policeman disappeared. Mr Punch was bouncing around the stage being very pleased with himself, when a clown came on with a great string of sausages and did a sausage dance. Then Mr Punch, naturally, hit *him* over the head with his stick, and stole the sausages and did a sausage dance.

While he was doing this, amid much clapping from the audience, a huge crocodile came on behind him and everyone was shouting, 'It's behind you!' – and the crocodile tried to eat the sausages and then to eat Mr Punch, but after a big fight, Mr Punch killed the crocodile. But after that, having been bitten a good deal, Mr Punch said he wasn't feeling very well, so he went to see a doctor, and the doctor tried to cure him with various medicines, and as these didn't work, he started hitting Mr Punch with a stick. Mr Punch started to hit him back until the Doctor was dead as well – and then the Policeman reappeared and hit Mr Punch on the head from behind – and then a jailor with a great big axe came on and chopped Mr Punch's head off. (More burying of heads in sweaters and running around the room.)

Finally the devil appeared and took Mr Punch down to hell, with, Perdita thought, some very good crepe paper flames. But of course Mr Punch had to fight with the devil and this was such a big fight that it nearly ended in the whole show being knocked over. But Mr Punch won (cheers) and that was the end of the play – and all the characters came back to life and took a bow, and Dan came out from behind the curtain, looking very hot indeed.

Everyone clustered around Dan, to congratulate him, and to get a closer look at the puppets – except for Perdita, whose head was, as they say in the books, whirling – and Sebastian. Perdita knew him very well, and she could see that he was trying to work something out.

Granny was looking at him, too, but she didn't know him quite so well. 'Not too violent for you?' she said. 'It was for me.'

'It's not that,' Sebastian said. 'I just don't quite understand how he managed to work three or four puppets at the same time, when he's only got two hands.'

'We'd better get some more logs in,' Uncle Mike said, 'before it gets too dark.'

'Yes, we're getting pretty low,' said Uncle Zac, who, Perdita thought, had been feeding the fires almost all day, but Uncle Zac was the kindest and mildest Uncle, and Perdita watched him go with some sympathy.

She wandered out into the hallway wondering vaguely what she might do next, and her eyes went to the log pile inside the big porch, or at least, where the pile used to be. All Uncle Zac's efforts that day had left only two or three layers of logs, and in the furthest corner, he had uncovered a box. She walked across and looked at it. It was black, oblong, with flat sides, and about the size of two shoeboxes. The wood, although it might have been varnished and polished once upon a time was stained by years of logs resting on it.

She looked at it, and it slowly occurred to her that there was a small keyhole in one side, near the top, and that keyholes were actually very interesting, and she ran across the hall and down the corridor, and through the baize door to the kitchen. Kettles were being boiled, and Aunty Rill was explaining to Dancing Perdita that carp were good eating, but they had pin bones, like salmon, that you had to get out, so it was a bit fiddly, and it was probably not a good idea to get a bone stuck in the throat of one of her nieces or nephews, so she was being incredibly careful.

The bunch of keys was where she had left it, and she took them and ran back to the box. She wriggled it out of its place – it was almost stuck to the tiles by a sort of glue made of old sawdust and wood resin, and squatted beside it.

The third key she tried fitted, and, much to her surprise, when she turned it, it turned easily, with a soft click. She put her thumbs against the side of the lid and pushed, but the lid didn't move.

Daddy, who, she realised, had been watching her from the living room doorway said, 'What have you got there? The magic box?'

She nodded. 'But it won't open.'

So they took it into the kitchen, and Daddy wiped it down, and got a flat-bladed knife, and pried around the lid until, with a sort of sigh, it opened. Inside, almost filling the box, was an embossed toffee tin. Daddy carefully slid it out onto the worktop. It rattled. Daddy applied the knife again, and the lid came off. He put the knife down and straightened up. 'All yours,' he said. 'You found it.'

Perdita knew that she was supposed to have trembling fingers for dealing with long lost treasure, but her fingers didn't tremble a bit.

Inside the box there was a neatly folded piece of paper, three monochrome photographs that looked as fresh and clear as if they had just been taken, and a small but very thick book barely 10cm square, with the words *My Diary 1943* embossed in gold. And three coins, a 1943 Three Pence piece, a rather worn One Shilling coin from 1920, and a big brown 1935 Penny. Perdita read the words around its edge: GEORGIVS V DEI GRA BRITT OMN REX FID DEF IND IMP. The Three Penny piece had a younger head, and the words GEORGIVS VI.

The photographs were of two girls and a baby who was sitting in a toy car. In the background of one of them was the terrace and the Grange.

Perdita unfolded the paper. It was headed:

The Grange, Tolpuddle
Dorset

And at an angle across the top left hand corner:

Telephone: Tolpuddle 23

The writing was extremely neat, written in purple ink which had, Perdita guessed, faded.

31/12/1943

> Dear Somebody in the Future,
> I am hiding my diary for this year, 1943, ~~so that if anyone reads it~~
> so that now you are reading it you will see what life is like this year. Jenny says that your money will probably be different in a hundred years so I am enclosing some money from my moneybox so you can see what it was like. I was going to enclose some chocolate too but I think that would be a waste.
> Love from
> Leonora Maria Martindale Hughes

Perdita picked up the diary and looked at Daddy.

'Do you think we ought to read it?' she said. 'It's not meant for us.'

'I don't think she'd mind if you read just a little bit,' Daddy said. 'In fact, I think she'd be rather pleased. We'll leave it for the Colonel tomorrow, but we could have a little nibble. Perhaps just the bits from this time of the year.'

Perdita opened the diary. The first page read, **Diary of Leonora Hughes, age 10**, and there was a sketch of a flower. All the following pages were full, tightly packed with very small, and still very neat writing. Perdita read some bits.

Saturday, 18th December

A very strange thing happened today. The telephone rang today and the operator told Mummy that it was Auntie Lillian from Tyneham but when Mummy said hello there was nobody there. And so Mummy asked the operator to ring back, and the operator came back after a long time and said that she was sorry but there was no such number. Mummy is worried.

Monday, 21st December

We had a letter from Auntie Lillian saying that she had moved into her new flat in Dorchester last Thursday and not to try to ring her at Tyneham because of something that was secret for the war effort.

Thursday, 24th December 1943
Christmas Eve

Mummy read out some very sad news, that Mrs Potter the writer of The Tale of Peter Rabbit died on 22 December. But she also read out a very funny letter from Daddy, with little pictures of palm trees. We are not allowed to know where he is, but Mummy thinks it is Italy.

Friday, 25th December 1943
Christmas Day

Mummy gave us some presents from Daddy, and said that he might be home in February that would be fun. We had a chicken for lunch, and Mummy said we were very naughty and mustn't tell anyone because of the rations.

Another very strange thing happened tonight. I am having a very exciting Christmas. I looked out of my bedroom window after we had gone to bed, to look at the stars, and I thought I saw two horses galloping through the sky, but Mummy said I was dreaming.

Monday, 28th December 1943
Childermass

It is raining again. We have very exciting news today. Some more officers are going to be billeted here at the beginning of January. It is all very secret, but it is nice because the house has seemed very empty since the last people left in November.

'What's Childermass?' Perdita said.

'The feast of the Holy Innocents,' Daddy said. 'You remember that when King Herod was looking for Jesus, he killed all the little boys in Bethlehem. It's not something most people think about much at Christmas.'

Perdita put the note and the coins and the diary back in the box, and thought about Titty on top of Kanchenjunga wanting to put the box back under the cairn, and saying that the people who put it there meant it to stay for a thousand years. But perhaps, as Daddy said, Leonora would have wanted her to read it.

Daddy smiled at her, and nodded slightly, and Perdita knew that he knew exactly what she was thinking, which he often did, so she put the lid back on the tin, but loosely, and walked slowly off to the library.

Chapter 21

Which is Not What Anybody Expected

By bath time, Perdita felt that she knew Leonora Maria Martindale Hughes really rather well, and would not have been altogether surprised had she met her in the corridor. She had meant to read just a little of the diary, but she had found herself (sitting by the library fire) turning the neat pages and dipping here and there, and she occasionally felt that Leonora was watching her, in a kindly sort of way.

She now knew that Leonora had a sister, Jenny, and a baby brother called Duncan. She knew that they lived in the two rooms above the kitchen, while for most of the year they had Important Officers billeted with them. Leonora didn't say very much about what was happening in the war. Even when a plane nearly crashed onto the lawn, she obviously felt that she shouldn't write much about it in case the Enemy somehow got hold of her diary. And she loved her younger sister, Jenny, and she really didn't like her new little brother very much. Perdita felt a little sorry for Duncan, because it wasn't his fault that he was a younger brother.

But Perdita knew that food was short, and that Leonora hated wartime food, such as oatmeal sausage, which had nothing to do with sausage, and everything to do with oatmeal. In fact, there was quite a lot about food, and Perdita began to feel that Leonora was secretly rather proud of the fact that she knew a lot more about cooking and housekeeping than a young lady in her position normally would have done.

The half page about hard-boiled dried eggs was symbolic. Leonora had described, with obvious disgust, how you were supposed to take dried egg powder, reconstitute it, and then bake it in little bowls so that it came out like hard-boiled eggs. But a week later she mentioned how they had real eggs from the hens they kept, which were supposed to count against their rations. She hated mock crab, mock cream, mock oyster soup, mock lemon curd – without lemons. But perhaps her least favourite was stuffed pigeons.

And yet… She and Jenny still played tennis, and they swam in the ponds. In the books that Perdita had read about the war there were refugees, and children who had been sent away from the towns to the country where they had never seen cows before, or who had to live with people who were not very nice. But Leonora and Jenny seemed to have a very nice time, and the Important Officers were always giving them treats because they missed *their* daughters – although not knowing when your Daddy would come home wasn't so nice.

Her own Daddy had been reading bits of the diary as well, but in the end, he said they should put everything back into the box and leave it for the Colonel when they left in the morning. Which seemed to be a good idea.

~

Carp in batter with chips having been a complete success, with not a bone in sight, they were in the middle of bath time, and Perdita had just got out of the bath and wrapped her towel around her, and Dulcie had just jumped in, her when all the lights suddenly went out.

It was very black, and for a moment she felt that she had gone to another strange place, another world, and then she said, 'I'll get my torch, I know where it is.'

'Everybody OK?' That was Daddy, somewhere.

'No problem!' That was Uncle Mike, somewhere else.

Perdita groped through the doorway, hit her toe on the side of the bed, put her hand on her torch and switched it on and the world came back, and from then on, everything was little pools of light. She pointed the torch while Dulcie and Sebastian had quick baths, and then Grandprof came in, in his own pool of light and said that it was a power cut everywhere, and that the boiler had stopped working too, so everybody thought we'd better save light and heat by all sleeping downstairs in the living room – because, anyway, that's where Dancing Perdita and Tim and Dan were going to sleep, and it would save making the beds again.

So they got dressed, and trundled their duvets down the stairs. In the living room, Uncle Zac had put more logs on the fire, and the candles were lighted, and the chairs and sofas had been re-arranged into a half-circle around the fire, and all the sofa cushions and chair cushions from the playroom had been spread around the floor. Uncle Zac and Aunty Fee and the two very littles, Laura and Amelia, and Granny and Grandprof were going to sleep in the library, but everyone else was curled up in what seemed to Perdita to be heaps and lumps. There was a lot of laughing.

Then they played charades and Dancing Perdita and Tim mimed being a Christmas Tree, and Grandprof mimed being Father Christmas stuck in the Chimney, and Granny mimed cleaning the AGA.

Then Dulcie said she would do her party piece, and stood up in front of the fireguard and recited 'A Good Play':

'We built a ship upon the stairs
All made of the back-bedroom chairs…'

That led to Josie doing her tongue twister:

'Betty Baker bought some butter
But she said the butter's bitter
If I put it in my batter, it will make my batter bitter
But a bit of better butter will make my batter better
So 'twas better Betty Baker bought a bit of better butter.'

And *that* led to Aunty Rill and Daddy doing 'With Her head Tucked Underneath Her Arm', and Uncle Zac and Daddy doing 'And the Great Big Saw…'

'OK,' Mummy said. 'We need to start settling down. Thank you Zac,'

So Daddy sat down with a big book, which he didn't look at, and made himself comfortable, and said: 'Well, I've found a story all about Tolpuddle Grange one year long ago, when it was all snowy and rainy, and it all started on this very day. Now, Grandprof will tell you that today is called Childermass, and it is said to be a very unlucky day.'

'That's right, said Grandprof. 'Very unlucky. Nobody ever began any work today, or it would go wrong. You weren't even supposed to cut your fingernails or toenails or put new clothes on. And especially you must never start out on a journey!'

'So it's luck that it rained,' said Sebastian. He was curled up with his back to Uncle Mike's legs.

'But this story just goes to prove that there's an exception to every rule,' Daddy said. 'So this is all about a boy called Jack, and on this very day, as I said, he set out to seek his fortune. You see, poor Jack was an orphan and he had no Mummy and Daddy. He lived with the miller down at a place called Yearling's Bottom, down the river, but the miller and his wife were horrible to Jack, and made him work all day and all night, and they gave him only crusts to eat, and he slept in the attic with mice and rats running over him.

'His best friend was the cat who lived in the mill, and the miller was horrible to the cat, too, because the cat wasn't very good at catching mice. And his other best friend was the dog who lived at the mill, and the miller was horrible to the dog, too, because he wasn't very good at catching rats.

'Now, that Christmas was particularly cold and wet and miserable for Jack, because the miller and his wife had a huge Christmas dinner and didn't let him have ANY of it, and made him do all the fetching and carrying and the washing up, so he decided to run away and seek his fortune. He knew it was an unlucky day for going to seek your fortune, but he didn't care. So he said goodbye to the cat and the dog, and tied up everything he had in his handkerchief and tied it to the end of a stick – which shows how clever he was, because that's not an easy thing to do – and walked out of house. But the cat and the dog ran after him and they said, 'We're coming with you! You're the only thing that makes life bearable for us, so we'll come and seek your fortune with you. And you never know when you'll need friends.'

'So Jack was very pleased, and they set off into the rain. They just reached the gateway, when they met a cockerel. And the cockerel said, "Where are you going, Jack?" and Jack said, "I'm going with my friends the cat and the dog, to seek my fortune." And the cockerel said, "Can I come with you? Because I know that in three days time it will be the New Year, and the miller is planning to kill and eat me!" And Jack said, "of course!" and he and the cat and the dog and the cockerel went off into the rain.

'They had not gone far when they passed a goat, tied to a stake and the goat said, "Where are you going, Jack?" and Jack said, "I'm going with my friends the cat and the dog and the cockerel, to seek my fortune." And the goat said, "Can I come with you? Because I know that in three days time it will be the New Year, and my master is planning to kill and eat me!" And Jack said, "of course!" and he and the cat and the dog and the cockerel and the goat went off into the rain.

'They had not gone far when they passed a bull in a farmyard, and the bull said, "Where are you going, Jack?" and Jack said, "I'm going with my friends the cat and the dog and the cockerel and the goat, to seek my fortune." And the bull said, "Can I come with you?

Because I know that in three days time it will be the New Year, and the farmer is planning to kill and eat me!" And Jack said, "of course!" and he and the cat and the dog and the cockerel and the goat and the bull went off into the rain.

'So they walked and walked, and got very wet, and they walked past Turner's Puddle, and Briantspuddle, and Affpuddle … until they saw a light, and they walked towards it through the mud, and they came to this very house, Tolpuddle Grange! Now in those days, the house was in a very bad way: it was empty, and neglected, and starting to fall down, but there was a single light, high up in one wall. So the cockerel flew up and perched on the sill – and do you know what he saw? He saw a band of robbers! They had been using the old house as their headquarters and they had told all the villagers that the house was haunted so nobody dared to go there. And there were sacks and sacks and sacks of gold and the robbers were counting it.

'The cockerel flew down and told Jack, and Jack made a plan! All the animals stood together under the window and they started to make a huge noise! The bull bellowed and the goat charged the front door with his horns, and the cockerel flew up and flapped at the windows, and the dog growled and barked, and the cat screeched, and Jack shouted, "Police! Police!"'

'Oh, dear,' Mummy said. 'Everybody calm down. Sebastian, stop being a goat. Jake, come down!'

When order was restored, Daddy waited for a minute and then went on. 'Now, all this noise frightened the robbers, and they all ran out of the back door. Then all the friends, Jack and the cat and the dog and the cockerel and the goat and the bull, went in and made themselves comfortable, and got dry and had a nice supper.

'But Jack knew that the robbers wouldn't give up so easily, so he made another plan. He put the cat in the rocking chair in the kitchen, and the dog under the table in the dining room, and he put the goat up at the top of the stairs, and the bull in the cellar, and the cockerel flew up and perched on the roof, and they put all the lights out and waited.

'Now the robbers weren't very brave, and didn't want to go back into the house, but the Chief Robber didn't want to look like a coward, so he plucked up all his courage and went back into the house, and all the others waited outside. Nothing happened for a bit, and then they heard the Chief Robber go "Owwwww!" and then "Eeeeek!" and then there was a great thumping noise, and then the Chief Robber went "Oooooch!" and then there was a horrible noise from the roof, and the Chief Robber came running out of the house, straight past the rest of the robbers, and they ran after him and they didn't stop until they were on the other side of Tolpuddle.

'Then the Chief Robber sat down panting, and the other robbers said, "What happened?" and the Chief Robber said, "We're never going back again! The house is full of horrible people! I went into the kitchen and there was an old woman sitting in the rocking chair knitting, and she stuck her needles into me!" – And that was the cat and her claws! "Then I went into the dining room and there was a man having dinner and he stuck his fork into me!" – And that was the dog and his teeth! "Then I tried to go upstairs but there was a man with a great big broom, sweeping, and he knocked me down stairs!" – And that was the goat with his horns! "Then I went down into the cellar and there was a man chopping wood and he hit me with his axe!" – And that was the bull with his hooves! Then the Chief Robber said: "But what finished me off was that there was a giant on the roof shouting 'Chuck him up to meee! Chuck him up to meee!'" – And that was the cockerel!

'And so the robbers ran away and never came back, and Jack and his friends lived happily ever after, and used the gold to make the Grange just as nice as it is today!'

'I could play some settling down music,' Dan said, and he sat at the piano with a single candle, and they sang 'Silent Night', and 'In the Deep Midwinter', and 'Oh Little Town of Bethlehem', because they were the Christmas carols that were quietest.

Then Tim played his accordion very softly, and sang a song that was so Scottish that when he had finished, he had to explain what it was about.

'Hush ye, my bairnie
Bonny wee laddie
When you're a man
you shall follow your daddie.
'Lift me a coo,
And a goat and a wether,
Bringing them hame
To your minnie thegither.

'Hush ye, my bairnie
Bonny wee lammie

Routh o' guid things
Ye shall bring to your mammie
Hare frae the meadow
deer frae the mountain
Grouse frae the moorlan'
And trout frae the fountain.

'Hush ye, my bairnie
Bonny wee dearie
Sleep! come and close the een
heavy and wearie
Closed are the wearie een
rest ye are takin'
Sound be yer sleepin'
And bright be yer wakin."

But Perdita didn't mind exactly what it meant. The words drifted over her, and when she woke a little later, everything was quiet except for people breathing and snuffling. The two candles on the mantelpiece were still alight, and the fire was casting a soft light around the room. Perdita snuggled against Mummy's back, and thought that she had never been quite so comfortable and went back to sleep.

29 DECEMBER

Chapter 22

Which is the End of this Story and the beginning of the Next

They were woken up by Tim, who had stepped over all the sleeping piles of people, and taken the Land-Rover down to the river, and had come back with the news that the water had gone down, and you could drive across to Tolpuddle. There was a lot of mud and debris on the road, but you could get across if you were careful, or you could go down the valley and cross at Afpuddle, because the flood had gone down there too, and the stranded car had been rescued.

There was a lot of bleary (another word to add to the list of words that really said what it meant) washing of faces, and Granny put the kettles on and was wondering if people would like black tea or black coffee when there was a crunching and crashing noise and Susie and George on the tractor drove up to the front door and unloaded a can of milk.

They were drinking hot chocolate and tea and coffee, and the Uncles had loaded the cars again, when the Colonel drove up in his car that was even older and more battered than Grandprof's. He congratulated them on surviving the night, and Perdita gave him the box with Leonora's diary in it, and he opened it. Strictly speaking, his wise old eyes should have filled up, just for a moment, and he should have brushed away a tear and said, 'Thank you young lady,' in a broken voice, but all he said was, in a perfectly ordinary voice, 'Astonishing nobody found it before. Many thanks!' and he went off with Uncle Mike to inspect Dulcie's hole in the ceiling.

Then they said goodbye to everybody all over again, and they were just getting in the car, when Tim came onto the porch steps with his accordion and sang, very loudly, and not very accurately:

'Farewell and adieu, the Grange at Tolpuddle
Farewell and adieu to the snow and the rain.
For we're under orders for to drive back to England
But we hope we will see good old Tolpuddle again!'

They all waved, Auntie Rill roared away in her little car, and Granny and Grandprof went more sedately in their big red one. Uncle Mike was still trying to catch Max, so Mummy let in the clutch, and swung their car into line behind Grandprof.

'Wait! Stop a minute,' Perdita said. Mummy slowed down and stopped.

'What is it?'

'We've got to do this properly,' Perdita said. 'In the books, they always say, 'Goodbye, house, Goodbye garden. We had a lovely time and we'll come back soon!'

There was a pause. And then Daddy said, 'Sounds reasonable,' and they all turned round and waved to the house, and shouted 'Goodbye house, goodbye garden. We had a lovely time and we'll come back soon!'

And Mummy started the car again, and they drove down the drive and out into the lane, singing 'Spanish Ladies' at the tops of their voices.

~

And that was the end of that story – apart from the huge breakfast that they had from a greasy spoon café in a lay-by halfway home – when Daddy had a fried egg in a roll, and when he bit it, the egg squirted all over his trousers.

But three weeks later, just as Perdita was finishing her morning Maths lesson, the Postman delivered two letters. The first was addressed to her, and was in a rather elegant envelope made, Mummy said, of laid paper, which was expensive. Inside was another expensive-looking sheet, and another, small envelope which contained three small coins.

> *The Grange*
> *Tolpuddle*
> Dear Miss Detective,
> I felt that I should let you know how pleased we are that you unearthed my sister Leonora's 'time capsule', and Leonora has asked me to thank you. It is amazing that it was hidden there for all these years: Leonora is sure that she originally hid it in the cellar, and we think that it may have been moved when someone was clearing out the house, and it was left in the porch and accidentally covered with logs. But she remembers making up the bunch of keys and hiding it in the chimney: she and my sister Jenny

were playing pirates and so they collected all the old keys that they could find in the house, largely for old trunks. Then they hid it in the chimney, because they had read somewhere that that was the proper thing to do with keys and forgot all about them! The chimney has been cleaned several times since then, of course, and so we can only assume that either the chimney sweepers were not very thorough and didn't find them, or they did find them and simply left them there.

And so we are very grateful that you found that little book of memories. It especially reminded us of the mysterious way in which the Grange telephone would ring on the seventeenth of December (which it did the week before we met, incidentally), and the legend of the horses which gallop in the sky at Christmas.

It will be my sister Leonora's 90th birthday next month (our sister Jenny is, sadly, no longer with us) and we will raise a toast to you! My sister wishes you to have the coins that lay so long in the box, and we hope they will remind you of a happy week at the Grange.

Yours, very sincerely,

Duncan Martindale Hughes (Col.)

The second was a rather larger and more rough-and ready envelope, addressed to Perdita and Sebastian and Dulcie, and sealed with a lot of sticky tape – which was the Right Way to Do It. Inside were three small packets, and a letter written in what Mummy described as 'copperplate' handwriting – almost painfully neat to Perdita's eye. She had to wait for half an hour until Sebastian and Dulcie came in from playing on the Tump, and then they opened it together, and Perdita read it out.

Dear Perdita, Sebastian and Dulcie,
We are writing to thank you for your kindness at Christmas – not simply because Perdita and Sebastian came to see us through the snow, and that was a very nice thing to do – but because of what you and your family did for our Grandson George. Before he went home he hardly stopped talking about how nice you were to him, and it was the first thing that Dulcie said to him that made it alright. We are very grateful, because he has had rather a hard time, and just for one afternoon you made him feel welcome.
We would also very much like you and your parents to come to stay with us next summer while George is here. We have a holiday cottage which we would be happy for you to take for a week, with no charge. We do not want you to feel obliged, but it would be a very kind deed.
With very best wishes,
Martha and Susie
PS. Susie says that this is not a very good letter because I have started five sentences with the word 'we'. I hope you don't mind.
PPS. We enclose some little remembrances! Happy New Year.

And when they opened them, there was a yellow tractor for Sebastian that came in a box scarcely bigger than a matchbox; and a shiny silver horse brooch exactly the same as the strange white horse at Uffington, for Dulcie; and for Perdita, a sliver chain necklace, and hanging from it an intricately worked tiny horse and carriage.

'Little unremembered acts of kindness,' Daddy said. 'Always the best.'

THE SHEPHERDS' PLAY

THE SHEPHERDS' PLAY

Shepherd 1
Shepherd 2
Mack
Mack's Wife
Angel
Sheep and Stars

Scene: the Hills

S1: Gosh it's cold.

S2: I think it's going to snow.

S1: It's not fair, the way we have to stay out on the hillside with our sheep, when everyone else is down in the village, all warm and cosy.

S2: And I think it's going to snow. It's in the air.

S1: And there's something else going on. I heard that three strangers have been asking where they can find a new baby. I don't know, do you?

S2: No. And I think it's going to snow.

S1: Look there's somebody coming. Oh, no. It's Mack, the sheep-thief. We'd better keep a close eye on our sheep!

Enter Mack

Mack: Good evening, shepherds! It's a cold night, isn't it.

S2: I think it's going to snow.

S1: What do you want, Mack? Don't think you're going to steal any of our sheep. We're too clever for you.

Mack: I wouldn't dream of such a thing. I was just thinking of you up here on the hills, and how cold you must be, so I've bought you a hot drink.

S2: That's not like you, Mack.

Mack: Well, I was down in the village just now, and I passed a man and a woman with a donkey, and they were looking for somewhere to sleep. There was no room at the inn, but the innkeeper let them stay in his stable. The innkeeper's wife brought them hot drinks, and she was so kind that I thought I should be kind too.

S1: You did, did you?

Mack: So here I am, and here are the hot drinks.

S1: Well … it is a very cold night.

S2: I think it's going to snow. I'd like a hot drink. Thank you.

Mack: Would you like some? Go on.

S1: Oh, very well. (*Yawns.*) What sort of drink is it?

Mack: Just a sleeping potion. Goodnight!

The Shepherds lie down and sleep.

Mack: That should keep them quiet! Now, I fancy roast lamb for supper!

Grabs a lamb and exits.

Enter Angel

Angel: Wake up! Wake up! Come on, wake up! You must go down to Bethlehem to find the baby Jesus. You will find him lying in a manger. And someone has stolen one of your lambs.

S1: It must have been that villain Mack. Let's go to Bethlehem and get our lamb back.

S2: And then we'll find the baby Jesus. But I think it's going to snow.

The scene changes. Mack's house. Mrs Mack is holding the lamb.

Mrs Mac: This is a lovely lamb. What shall we do with it? I like roast lamb. Or stew perhaps?

Mac: I don't mind. I'll just take it outside and kill it!

S1 (*outside*): Mack, Mack! Where are you?

S2: We want our lamb back before it snows.

Mrs Mac: What shall we do? I know! I'll wrap it in this shawl and put it in the cradle. Now, lamb, lie there and be quiet!

She puts it in the cradle. S1 and S2 come in.

S1: Ok, where's the lamb?

Mack: I don't know what you're talking about.

Mrs Mac: There's no lamb here. You can search the house if you like.

They search.

Lamb: Baa.

S1: What's in that cradle?

Mrs Mack: My baby of course. He's got a bit of a cold. That's why he's going 'baa'.

S1: Oh, poor baby! Let me give him a cuddle.

Finds lamb.

Mrs Mack: Oh dear! My baby's turned into a lamb!

Enter Angel

Angel: Now peace to everyone. There is a real baby next door in the stable, and he would love to see the lamb.

S1: That would be lovely. We can give him the lamb as a present.

Mack and Mrs Mack: We'll come too!

Mack: It's going to be a wonderful night.

S2: If it doesn't snow.

The Books

A lot of books have been read by people in this book, and just in case you're wondering where some of the extracts come from, here's a list.

Also by Peter Hunt

Perdita and the May People

Perdita lives in a world full of books and stories, but real
life is just as full of strange things: dancing archaeologists,
paragliding grannies, maypoles and ancient wells and
strange music … and two more people called Perdita.
    And they all seem to be connected…

    This is the first of the Perdita novels.

Perdita and the Midsummer People

First there is a lady chained to a birch tree, and then
Perdita sees a huge White Horse where there isn't one,
and then there is a farmer ploughing dangerously close
to a fairy ring…
    And the wild Midsummer festivals are coming closer
and closer…

    This is the second of the Perdita novels, and the book
    includes a long short story: 'What Didn't Happen at
    Samhain'

Lightning Source UK Ltd.
Milton Keynes UK
UKHW020639040321
379777UK00010B/680